The Pathway Back

By

Hazel Goss

Published by Final Chapter Publishing

Fiction Statement
This novel is a work of fiction. Some of the events described really happened but the characters are the product of the author's imagination and do not represent actual persons, living or dead. Any resemblance is purely coincidental.

A CIP catalogue record of this book is available from the British Library.

ISBN: 978-0-9955576-3-5

To my daughter, Amanda and friend, Jean, for reading my manuscript and my husband, John, for his support and patience, with love.

The Prologue

1875

The *Daphne* creaked and groaned as she wallowed in the depths of a trough. Just as Jane wondered if the ship was going to lift herself up to take the next wave it rose, shaking and shuddering. The noise was terrifying. Jane was confined to her quarters where she stood, bracing herself, holding onto the black oak beam that the sand timer swung from. It loomed perilously close to her head but she needed to be central. If she allowed herself to be near the edge seasickness would overwhelm her.

The lantern swung, highlighting corners of the navigator's cabin. It was on the port side and contained a narrow cot bed, a table, usually covered in charts, a chair and, in deference to her, a metal bowl and pitcher. There was also a chamber pot that sat in a hole in a wooden structure, behind a curtain.

When the storm began she had stood the charts in the rack, taken everything that was not fixed and stowed it as best she could. But the pitcher, which was too large to go in a cupboard, rolled and clanged around the floor, adding to the noise of the wind and crashing waves.

Jane hated being confined to quarters. It made her feel trapped and now, in the midst of this violent storm, she wondered if she would ever reach England.

The voyage from Calcutta could take just four months but the winds had not been favourable and it was taking longer. Her thoughts of the warmth and comfort of her home in India were halted with the crack and groan of breaking wood, like a tree being felled. The ship lurched dangerously over to the port side.

Jane lost her grip on the beam and her flailing hand found the timer. She grabbed it as her feet slipped away from her. Were they sinking? The lantern swung so hard against the bulkhead it shattered. Everything was black. She could see nothing but she could feel cold water seeping into her boots.

'Mary, Mother of God, save me. Hail Mary, Hail Mary. I don't want to die' There was shouting just audible above the wind and the waves.

'Cut the stays! Get it overboard before we all go with it!' She could hear frantic chopping sounds and thanked God the sails had all been reefed.

Released from the weight of the mast hanging over the side, the ship righted herself. Jane cried with relief, opened her eyes and realised she could see. There was a glow coming from the sand timer. It was eerie. She wanted to release her grip on it but something held her.

There was a knock on her door.

'Come in,' she shouted, happy that someone could now tell her what was happening. Ben, the navigator, entered holding a lantern. The timer lost its glow and she realised it was just out of sand so she turned it over.

Ben bowed, noting her slim figure and curly auburn hair. She was an attractive woman and he had been a long time at sea. Jane was, however the owner's daughter and unobtainable so he just smiled and said, 'Thank you, m'lady. I was just coming to see you were not hurt and to check the timer but I see you have it all under control.' Jane nodded, feeling calmer now.

' I expect you guessed,' Ben continued, 'that we lost the main mast but with the other two we can make way but it'll be slow. We're also bailing.' He held the lamp lower. 'I'm surprised it's wet in here but I'll get a lad to mop it dry.'

He moved over to her table and sorted through the charts finally selecting one. He studied it for a while, then said, 'I'll work it out accurately but my estimate of our position and possible speed means we could get to Liverpool in a week. We've sustained a lot of damage but the cargo seems fine.' He turned to go, then stopped and hooked his lantern up, retrieving her broken one. 'Can't leave you in the dark. Goodnight m'lady.'

The *Daphne* limped into harbour six days after the storm, to be met by Jane's parents, Lord and Lady Marshall. She flew down the gangplank into her mother's arms and then hugged her father. He was pleased to see her but could see the damage to the ship. 'I'd better get aboard, dear, my *Daphne* looks a mess.'

The ladies stepped aside and while he investigated the damage they talked and talked, trying to fill the gap of six years since her marriage and voyage to India. Jane explained that her husband, Captain Cecil Carstairs, would come in a few months when he got leave from his regiment.

'We must make the most of the time we have together,' said her mother. 'As soon as you're rested from the journey we will throw a welcome home party.' Her mother hugged her again but then looked up as she saw her husband descending the gangplank looking serious. Several seamen, carrying Jane's trunk and other belongings, followed him.

'Come my dears let's get you home,' said Lord Marshall and he turned to Jane adding, 'I'm sure you must be exhausted after that storm.' He helped them up into the carriage and as they drove away from the harbour he told them the damage to *Daphne* was worse than he'd thought. 'I'll get a shipwright to assess it properly but I think she's made her last voyage. It would've been worse if I'd lost the cargo too but, amazingly, the tea kept dry.'

The carpenter agreed with Lord Marshall and the *Daphne* was to be broken up. Before that she was stripped of her assets and an auction was held. The whole family attended. There was brisk bidding for the sails, the sheets and the pulleys. Everything went under the hammer and eventually the sand timer was held up.

'Oh, Father, could I have that please? Jane asked, 'I held onto it when the ship heeled over and I feel it saved my life. Please?'

He smiled and held up his hand shouting, 'Sorry that's not for sale.'

Part 1

Chapter 1

December 2015

Dad rang Jason and his voice was more animated than usual. 'Jason have you seen the auction of the contents of Marshall Hall? It's tomorrow at 10 in the Hall itself. Shall we go?'

'I'll ask Catherine if she minds. I don't think we've any other plans.'

Jason knew Dad would be looking for toy cars. He'd collected them for years and loved the old metal clockwork ones and the valuable, boxed die-cast Dinky toys. Jason suspected his dad played with them when he was alone, reverting back to his childhood.

When Catherine returned from work she said she was more than happy for Jason to attend the auction. 'If you're out for a couple of hours I can clean the house and then we're free to go out in the afternoon or Sunday. We really ought to do some Christmas shopping.'

He nodded and rang his dad back and they agreed a time. 'Dad's picking me up at 9.00 so we can have a browse before it kicks off.'

The following morning Catherine was vacuuming the lounge as Dad's car drew up. It only took half an hour to drive to Marshall Hall so they had time to examine the catalogue and look at the lots.

There were large, beautiful cabinets made of warm walnut. There were also elegant occasional tables of polished mahogany and an enormous dining table of solid oak. The desire to pause, touch and trace the intricate pattern of the grain was strong, but Dad was on a mission. The smaller items were collected together and then they slowed, past china dolls, beautifully dressed with bloomers poking out from under lace-trimmed dresses, train sets, boxes of alphabet bricks and finally, toy cars.

'Look at that,' said Dad, 'A Heinz Big Bedford Van in excellent condition. They can be worth nearly £50. I'm going to bid for that. There's not much more of interest for me. Anything caught your eye?'

'I saw a sand timer, almost certainly off a ship, but I'm not going to bid much for it. Wouldn't want to upset her indoors. Jason denied having his dad's collecting mania but being a keen dinghy sailor he did have a cabinet at home with a few nautical objects. He had a telescope, binoculars, a compass and a sextant.

The auction was about to begin so they took their seats and waited, patiently. Once it began they stayed still and silent, anxious not to make any move that might send a signal to say they were bidding. When the Heinz van appeared Dad sat up and when the price paused at £30 he raised his hand.

'Thirty five pounds, forty now on the Internet,' said the auctioneer, his eyes sweeping across the room. Dad raised his hand again. 'Forty-five in the room.' There was a pause, then, 'Forty-five, any more? Then it's sold to the gentleman on my right.' His gavel banged down and Dad beamed with delight.

They sat through endless pieces of china and tableware until Jason began to fidget and whispered he'd be happy to leave.

'What about that sand timer?'

'Not sure I can be bothered.' Just as he said that the timer was held aloft. Jason grinned at his dad and sat up, alert, to see what bids were being made. It seemed there was little interest and he bought it for just twenty-five pounds.

'Well, we've had a good morning,' said Dad, when they emerged into the grey, chill air. 'Let's celebrate. Would you prefer a beer or coffee?' Jason shivered and fastened his jacket. 'Coffee sounds good.'

They entered the coffee shop, relaxing into the warmth and Dad found a seat while Jason queued. He returned with a tray, two large frothy coffees and two scones with cream and jam. 'Sorry it took so long. These coffee shops are definitely not fast food.'

Dad laughed, 'I don't mind waiting when you come bearing scones, clotted cream too, my favourite.'

They ate and drank with just an occasional remark until Dad finished, sighed with pleasure and looked into his plastic bag to find his Heinz van. He handled it carefully, opened the box and took it out. 'I can't believe any boy ever played with this. It's in pristine condition, no chips or dints, beautiful.' As he put it back in its box he said, 'Let's look at your timer.'

Jason pulled up his bag. 'It's quite heavy,' he said and watched, almost mesmerised as the sand ran down. Dad held out his hand and Jason passed it to him.

'It is heavy. There's writing and symbols on the bottom. He held it closer, 'It says, *Daphne*. That's quite clear but the symbols are too tiny, probably the craftsmen's mark.' He nodded his approval and handed it back. Jason glanced at the name and, as he stowed it back into its bag, he said, 'I could look up *Daphne* and see what I can find out about her.'

There was no time to do that when he got home. Catherine barely glanced at the timer, when he showed it to her, being eager to have lunch and go Christmas shopping. They traipsed around Harrogate until they were exhausted but it had been a successful trip. They took bulging bags, with rolls of wrapping paper sticking up from one, back to the car.

That evening was spent wrapping and labelling and they went to bed happy and satisfied with their day.

Jason went to sleep immediately but woke up several hours later anxious and sweating. He laid still and the dream replayed.

He was in a cabin of an old sailing ship, bucking and shaking noisily in a storm. There was a woman, holding on tight and he could feel her fear. She needed help and he seemed to be keeping her safe until the ship began to come upright again. Then he let her go.

She survived the storm. He knew that because now he saw her, through leaded glass panes, in a large room. It was a library, with books from floor to ceiling in cabinets and some on open shelves. A fire was crackling in a huge fireplace with a marble surround and mantelpiece. On the wall above it was a portrait of a gentleman holding a model ship in his right hand while his left hand rested on a large globe.

The woman sat in an armchair close to the fire. Her auburn hair concealed her face as she leant forward caressing a white greyhound.

3

The dog was in stark contrast to her black clothes. Jason could hear her crying and felt a wave of desire to help her, as he had on the ship, but was frustrated and powerless.

Jason woke up and his dream faded as he thought of the next day, Sunday. There was no rush to get up, a chance to sleep longer and with that thought he slept until morning, without dreaming.

They got up late and had a large brunch of bacon, sausage, egg and tomatoes with toast and coffee.

'That was really yummy. I'm so full I won't want to eat again for at least half an hour,' said Jason.

Catherine grinned at him. 'Well you'll need all that energy because we've got to get the Christmas tree out of the loft and decorate it today. It's no good you making that face. We've invited Phil, Jenny, Emily and Sean, Carol and what's-his-name from next door, to our party in just a couple of days. So it really has to be done today.'

'Mike, that's his name. It'll be a good chance to get to know them a bit better. OK. I'll make a start now unless you want me to load the dishwasher.'

'Let's leave that for now and I'll help you.'

She stood at the bottom of the loft ladder whilst Jason went up and handed down the artificial tree, in three sections, swathed in several bin bags and then two boxes of decorations. They took it all into the lounge, unpacked the tree and Jason put it together. 'Right, that's my job done. The artistic bit's yours.'

'OK, but will you test the lights before you leave me to it?'

He plugged in the red ones and they blinked obligingly. The white ones played 'Jingle Bells' and Catherine giggled. 'It'll be a bit much to have that playing all day. Can you find the silent mode?' He nodded but they had to hear the beginning of a very tinny rendering of 'White Christmas' and 'The Holly and the Ivy' before he found it.

'Right. I'm going to load the dishwasher and then check my emails.'

Catherine nodded and became absorbed in winding the strings of lights, fixing the star on the top so the last light shone through it and hanging baubles. Many of them had memories. The shiny metal Santa had come from a shop in New York, a wooden soldier from Holland and the glass icicles they'd bought from a stately home in

4

the Cotswolds. There were also little, messy snowmen made of toilet rolls and cotton wool and cardboard stars with glued glitter, made by the children at the nursery. She had spent two weeks there, when she was at school, gaining experience of life in the work place but realised it was not going to be what she wanted to do.

Catherine now worked for a cycle parts distribution company where the work was absorbing and sometimes challenging. She was pleased to have used her few days of holiday left to extend her Christmas holiday. Sometimes she resented Jason having so many long school breaks, leaving him in bed while she went to work. It was a good feeling to have days ahead without any work issues to think about.

Finally she stood back to put the last piece of tinsel in place and called Jason to lift it for her into the large bay window. When he had done that she plugged in the lights and they stood close together admiring it. He put his arm around her and she snuggled into him.

'Somehow it doesn't feel like Christmas until the tree's glowing in the window,' she said.

Catherine spent the rest of the afternoon cooking for the party and then dinner that evening. Jason helped with some vegetables and they ate in front of the television contented with the day.

'I think we should have a cheers moment,' he said, holding his glass of Merlot up to the twinkling lights of the tree.

'What are we drinking to?'

'Two weeks off school stroke work and to a happy Christmas seeing friends and family.' As they clinked glasses and sipped their wine, he added, 'and to getting just a little tipsy and having sex with my gorgeous wife tonight.' She smiled and raised her glass again, saying huskily, 'I like the second toast more than the first.'

The evening was short as they went to bed early and both, eventually, slept without moving or dreaming until morning.

Chapter 2

Catherine yawned, stretched then sat up abruptly in bed. 'Oh my God! Wake up Jason, look at the time.'

'What? Oh, it's 10 o'clock. What's wrong with that? It's the holidays and we've had a great lie-in.'

She flounced out of bed, shivered and put on her thick dressing gown. Her hair, tangled and messy, seemed to indicate an irritable mood so he made the effort to sit up and look alert. 'So what's the problem?'

'The party, it's tonight. We need to tidy, clean, shop for fresh veg and I need to do my hair and my nails.'

'Right, then delegate; give me specific jobs and you do yours. No need to panic.'

'I'm not panicking, just anxious. I'll make some tea and then write a his and her's list.'

An hour later Jason was in the supermarket with a list of salad items, vegetables, fruit, bread and wine. The shop was playing Christmas songs and he hummed along happily as he filled his trolley.

'That looks a healthy selection. I hope there's going to be something wickedly bad for us too.'

'Hi Phil, said Jason looking at his friend with a grin. 'Don't worry, from what I've seen going on in the kitchen, Catherine's organising quite a spread.'

'I'm looking forward to it. Who else is coming? Anyone I know?'

'No, although I think you met Jenny, our part time PE teacher, at that fun run we organised last year.'

'Yes, little, cute and fit.'

Jason nodded, 'She's also divorced and possibly lonely, so be nice to her.'

'I'm always nice. Anyway I'm holding you up and we can chat tonight. See you, seven thirty.'

Phil strode away and Jason hoped he hadn't appeared to be match making, although he was. Jenny had a great sense of humour but since her divorce she seemed weighed down and stressed. Someone like Phil, dependable, kind and also divorced, would be ideal.

Jason had met Phil at university and they had been dinghy sailing buddies for years. He pulled himself up from his daydream when his phone signalled a text. He read, 'Make it four red and three white, please.'

Catherine's timing was perfect because he had just arrived at the wine section. There was a special offer on his favourite Merlot and, as he didn't like white, he chose a 'Gavi', middle-of-the road in price, and hoped for the best. He pushed the laden trolley to the checkout, paid then ran through the drizzle to the car and loaded the boot. His head was filled with carols and he was looking forward to being host that evening.

When he got home Catherine pounced on his purchases and whisked them into the appropriate cupboard while making approving noises. He made some coffee and whilst the machine was burbling he looked at the jobs list. 'My goodness you must have been whizzing round whilst I was shopping. Nearly all your jobs are ticked, only paint nails left.'

'Yes but there will be some cooking to do later. Those were just my morning jobs. I'm going to do my nails now whilst we have that coffee. It smells delicious.'

'I'm not sure I've time for coffee. There're still several items on my list. Make sure white wine is chilled and red breathing, move the chairs in the lounge, lay the table in the dining room with Christmas cloth and heat up the dish warmers.'

'Nothing that can't wait till later, Jason. I'm sorry I was snappy this morning. Sit with me and chat for a minute.' He did as she suggested, relaxing into the lighter atmosphere. He told her about meeting Phil and his mention of Jenny, and asked if she thought he should have mentioned her divorce.

'I don't think she makes a secret of it. Anyway we can't make them fall for each other, just give them a chance to meet and talk.'

The rest of the day passed quickly and by 7.30, when the first guests arrived, they were ready. During the pre-dinner drinks, Jason discovered that his new neighbours, Carol and Mike, used to dinghy sail but had not yet looked for a local club. They were also interested in buying a boat. That set the conversation going with great enthusiasm leaving the non-sailors floundering. They sipped their drinks and hoped for an opportunity to change the subject. Jenny was one of those so she braved the kitchen and offered to help, just when Catherine needed another pair of hands.

'Oh, yes please. Would you load these two tureens with carrots and peas. I'll do the roast potatoes and parsnips. Is everything going well in there?'

'They're talking sailing, which is why I came to help. I don't know what a broad reach is or a sheet. It has a language of its own.'

'Yes, I know how you feel. I went on a sailing course with Jason before we were married. It turned out I was the only complete novice so the instructor went extremely fast so as not to bore everyone else and I struggled to keep up. On the last day he announced we were to have a race. I said I didn't want to but everyone was in couples and if I didn't then Jason couldn't. We set off and everything went wrong. It was blowing quite hard. We began to argue and, as I was at the helm, all faults were mine. I shouted I'd had enough so I let go of the main sheet and the rudder and folded my arms.' She began to laugh at the memory. 'The sails flapped, the boat rocked from side to side and the rescue boat hurtled towards us. I have to say we were very nearly divorced before we were married over that!'

'I can just picture it,' said Jenny giggling. 'Are we ready to take everything in?' Catherine nodded. They carried the steaming dishes in and placed them on the table and then Catherine invited everyone to come and eat.

When the business of loading plates was completed Catherine turned to Sean and asked if they had any holidays booked.

'Well, we've hired a yacht to go sailing in a flotilla around the Greek islands. We've been saving up for this and we're going in April, before it gets too hot and before...' He paused and looked at his wife, Emily.

She nodded and said, 'He stopped because he wasn't sure if he should tell you all that I'm pregnant.'

There was a flurry of congratulations. No one at the party had children yet, but they were all delighted for Emily and Sean.

Catherine had hoped to change the subject by asking about holidays and this revelation did just that. Carol and Mike said they'd thought about having a baby, now they'd bought their first house but needed to save some money first to manage on one wage. Jason nodded but said nothing and Catherine hugged herself inwardly, knowing there was a strong possibility she was pregnant too. She had not even told Jason she had missed a period but she had booked an appointment with her doctor the following day and bought a pregnancy testing kit, but hadn't used it yet.

When everyone had gone home they loaded the dishwasher and went to bed feeling happy that it had been a lovely evening.

They finished clearing up the following morning and then Catherine went upstairs to make the bed, shower and get dressed. She came down forty minutes later and looked for him but he was not in the lounge. 'Jason? Where are you? Oh, you made me jump – thought you were in the lounge.'

'Sorry, I was in the den.'

'You weren't working with just two days to go before Christmas, were you?'

She looked radiant, he thought, the light from the front door gleaming on her auburn hair swinging just on her shoulders. He resisted the temptation to remove her coat and other clothes to admire the whole, slim beauty. Anyway it would have been pointless because she would have stopped him.

'Where are you going?' he asked.

'That's why I was looking for you, to say I'm going to the doctors.'

He frowned. 'You never said yesterday. What's wrong?'

She laughed. 'Nothing. That's why I didn't say anything. It's just a check up at something called the 'Well Woman Clinic'. Anyway I'll only be half an hour or so.' She added a scarf to her coat, kissed him on the cheek and went out.

Jason went back into the den and finished wrapping her Christmas present. It was a Fit-bit with a purple strap. He loved his and hoped it would encourage her to do more exercise. This was the problem with being a PE teacher. You knew the importance of exercise and how good it made you feel and you wanted everyone else to enjoy it too. He added a small gold bow to the parcel and wrote on the tag, 'Love you forever, Jason,' then hid it in the desk drawer. He checked his emails and agreed with Phil that they'd give the frostbite sailing session a miss. Finally he cleared his inbox and junk. What should he do next?

His watch said Catherine had been out for half an hour so he would put the kettle on and see if there was a rosé chilling in the fridge for later. As the kettle hummed he wandered back into his study and looked at his collection of nautical memorabilia. He would have to give that sand timer a clean before he showed Phil. It looked dull sitting between the gleaming brass telescope and compass. He decided to Google *Daphne* and see what he could find out. As he sat back at the computer the kettle clicked off but he ignored it, waiting for Catherine to come home.

The search revealed *HMS Daphne* (1838) and he wondered if it had been that one. There was also a *Lady Daphne* but that was a Thames barge. He dismissed that, feeling sure the engraver would not have missed the word, 'Lady' off. It seemed too difficult, with so little information, to establish exactly which *Daphne* his timer came from.

Jason looked at his watch. She said she would be just half an hour but it was now an hour and a half. He felt anxious and tried to rationalise his fear. She'd probably popped to the supermarket, although they had planned to get a takeaway later. Where was she? Perhaps he should ring the doctors.

The doorbell rang. He opened it to two policemen. 'Mr Brownlow I am Sergeant Mullins and this is Constable Jones. Would you mind if we came in? I'm afraid we've got some bad news.'

They told him she was crossing the road from the doctors, had slid on the ice and a van was unable to stop in time. The impact killed her instantly.

Jason found it hard to take in what they were saying. How could his beautiful, vibrant wife be dead?

The police offered to contact a relative or friend and he was able to give his dad's number. Constable Jones stayed with him until Dad arrived and then left after leaving contact details.

Jason sat, head in his hands, crying and shaking uncontrollably.

'I'm going to phone the doctor,' said Dad.

Jason looked up, squinting though swollen lids. 'I don't need a doctor. I need Catherine.'

'I know son, I know. But at the moment you can't cope and there are lots of things we must do and I can't do it alone.'

The doctor came and wrote a prescription for sleeping pills and more pills to dull his emotions. 'I've only given you five sleeping pills because I don't want you to get hooked but between Christmas and New Year the surgery is open and, if you're desperate, I can give you some more. The other one I've put on repeat and you must take it every day and not stop taking it until we've discussed it.' He looked at Dad, assuming Jason had not been listening, being so wrapt in his misery.

'I'll be staying here for a while so I'll make sure he follows your instructions, Doctor. Thank you for coming.' He saw the doctor to the door and then returned to Jason. 'I've got to go to the chemist and get this prescription. Will you be all right for half an hour, or would you like me to call Phil?'

'No, please don't tell anyone yet. I'll just sit here. You go.'

Jason had a drug induced sleep that night but his eyes were still puffy when he pulled himself up on one elbow to sip the tea Dad had brought. It was silent at first and then Dad spoke gently. 'We have to register the death and make arrangements for the funeral. This has to be done today because it's Christmas Day tomorrow.'

Jason nodded. 'Ok I'll get up. Don't make me breakfast but have some yourself. I'm not hungry.'

Dad put on a pot of coffee and made toast hoping the smell of both would make Jason feel hungry.

'That coffee smells good.' Dad smiled as Jason poured a cup and sat opposite him. He pushed the plate of toast towards him and was gratified when Jason took a piece.

The day was spent ringing to make appointments and then attending them. They discovered that no cremations could take place until after New Year's Day and even then the first slot was on the seventh of January, in the morning. It was going to be a long, sad Christmas break.

That evening Dad cooked the gammon joint Catherine had bought and made them a meal but neither of them had much appetite because they were both suffering grief and exhaustion.

It was Christmas Day. Church bells were ringing and all over the country children were waking early, excited to see what Santa had brought. Mothers were cooking oversized turkeys and the air was full of delicious smells and the sound of carols.

In Jason's house there were just two miserable people.

'I know what to do today,' said Dad. Let's remove all traces of Christmas. We can't celebrate it so let's remove it.'

Jason found the box that had contained tree lights and decorations and began to dismantle the tree, tears running down his cheeks as he did so remembering their pleasure when they erected it. Dad helped him and then they returned it all to the loft.

'I can't see me ever using it again. How can Christmas ever be a celebration when it will be the anniversary of the worst day of my life?'

'I feel the same but who knows what the future may hold. Let's just cross this one off, although I think we should open our presents.

He offered Jason a small packet, which he opened, reluctantly. It was a pair of navigation dividers. 'Thanks, Dad; I'll it add to my collection. You'd better open yours.'

Dad fumbled with the parcel and a beautiful, soft, angora jumper spilled onto his lap. 'I assume Catherine chose this. It's lovely. I wish I could thank her.' He stood up abruptly and went into the kitchen. 'I'll make us a sandwich,' he said, his voice high and breathy with emotion.

Jason felt a wave of anger. He scooped up Catherine's presents, went into the study and added his one to the pile then took them through the kitchen out into the garden to the rubbish bin. Dad was making tea and Jason mumbled, 'Just couldn't stand to look at them any longer.'

The rest of the Christmas break passed excruciatingly slowly. Dad organised a lunch after the funeral, at a local hotel and they went for long walks. Eventually Jason was able to inform friends and family, mostly by email. Cards and flowers began to arrive and Dad fielded all the phone calls. Jason was deeply grateful for his help.

Chapter 3

Phil couldn't stop thinking about Jenny. She'd been very quiet when they'd been talking about sailing at the party but she was not shy and happily chatted about her two nephews when the subject turned to children. At that point he'd been quiet because he knew nothing about kids. His brief marriage had been unproductive and his divorce acrimonious. It had made him wary of forming another attachment but he liked Jenny and really wanted to know her better.

When they'd all been tipsy, towards the end of the evening, there had been a wonderful feeling of bonhomie and someone suggested they exchanged phone numbers and email addresses. It was quite chaotic as everyone produced their phones asking for numbers and surnames to be repeated but it did mean he could contact her.

He sat at his computer and hesitated. It was harder than he thought. Supposing she had been totally underwhelmed. He clicked on mail, saw he had one email and opened it.

Hello Phil, I just wanted to say it was fun at Catherine and Jason's last night and wondered if you'd like to have a coffee or drink with me some time.
Cheers,

Jenny

He grinned with delight and replied immediately.

Hi Jenny, I was on the point of emailing you! Are you busy tomorrow night?

He pressed send and before he'd even stood to put the kettle on there was an answer.

It's Christmas Eve and I'm driving to my Mum's. What R U doing now? Fancy meeting at the Duck and Drake, 8ish?

He did, replied immediately and went to have a shower. As he lathered and sang an old Beatles song, 'She loves you yeh, yeh…..' he wondered if she liked his type of music, read similar books, liked the same films. There was so much to discover, apart from the allure of her petite body. He looked down at his own, frowning at the excess tummy fat. Perhaps a diet would be in order, after Christmas.

Jenny was sitting on a bar stool nursing a white wine when he arrived and smiled a welcome showing perfect white teeth. He struggled not to kiss her immediately.

'What are you drinking?' she asked.

'I'll have a pint of lager, please, not fussy which one.'

She attracted the attention of the barman and when she'd paid for the drink they moved to a table that had just become vacant. It was quieter and now they could talk.

'Cheers.' Phil raised his glass and she clinked hers to it. 'To a happy Christmas that started so well with us meeting properly for the first time.' He sipped his drink. 'So you're going to your Mum's for Christmas. Is it far?'

'No, only Ripon but all the family are coming, twelve in all, so I've promised to help with the preparations. What are you doing?'

He made a rueful grin. 'I'm just spending it quietly on my own.'

She looked horrified. 'No!' came out rather loudly. People turned to look at her. She giggled, embarrassed and whispered, 'You can't be alone at Christmas. Haven't you any family?'

'My parents split up when I was eighteen and at Uni. I knew it was likely but I still found it hard. Mum now lives with a man called Jake that I don't get on with and Dad moved to France and lives with a woman called Michelle. She's OK and I got an invitation to spend Christmas with them but they're very touchy feely and it makes me uncomfortable. No siblings either, before you ask.'

'Oh. Have you had Christmas on your own before? I'd hate it.'

Phil laughed and explained that he now enjoyed the chance to relax and do exactly what he wanted, watch his choice of TV and eat a steak instead of turkey.

'But if you normally live on your own what makes Christmas special?' she asked.

He shrugged, 'Well when you put it like that, nothing, although I do like those ancient films full of sloppy romance. You know, Bing Crosby crooning, 'White Christmas' and all that.'

She smiled. 'Would you like to have Christmas day with my family and me? It's likely to be a bit manic because my sister has twin boys, aged four. They can get over excited but Christmas is really for children, isn't it?'

'Wouldn't your Mum have something to say about that?'

'She's more likely to be cross with me for not bringing you and allowing you to be alone on Christmas day! So what do you say?'

He grinned, 'Thank you, I'd like that.'

'Good, I'll ring her right now but I'll have to pop out for a minute because it's too noisy in here.' He nodded and watched her little figure wiggle between the tables and out of the door. It was daunting to meet her parents and her family all at once, when this was their first date but he could cope. It would be worth it just to see more of Jenny. She returned and signalled she was going to the bar to get more drinks but he shook his head so she came straight over. 'Don't you want another?'

'Yes but it's my shout.' He stood up as she sat down. 'So what did your mum say about having another mouth to feed?'

'She said, and here I quote, "Oh good, I thought I'd gone over the top with the size of the turkey and vegetables, not to mention the pudding and mince pies. The more the merrier."'

'That's lovely. Same again and then we can make arrangements?' She nodded and smiled happily when he returned with the drinks.

'I've plenty of space in my car but we can't put you up which would mean me bringing you home....'

'And then you couldn't have a drink. No I'm not worried about alcohol. I'll need my wits to make a good impression on your family. If you give me the address and a time to arrive I'll bring myself.'

They left the Duck and Drake together, shivering in the cold wind. Phil offered to walk her home but she refused, knowing it was in the wrong direction for him.

Christmas day loomed dull and overcast, but Phil didn't care. He was looking forward to experiencing a traditional family event instead of being alone and lonely.

Jenny had said Christmas jumpers were essential. For the first time he was glad he had bought one a couple of years ago.

He showered and dressed smartly and then lowered the tone with a, 'Ho, Ho, Ho laughing Santa with a fluffy beard', jumper. He had time to make a few phone calls before he left and sat with a cup of coffee to call his mother and then his father. Having done that duty he thought of calling Jason but decided it wasn't necessary having wished him and Catherine a lovely Christmas when they'd been at the party. He'd chat to him after Christmas when he would have more to tell him.

Phil rang the bell of Jenny's parents' house and Jenny flung open the door and hugged him. Luscious smells assailed his nostrils and he was immediately enveloped with the warmth of the log fire and the welcome. Everyone was smiling, the two children happily playing on the floor with a wooden train set that extended into almost every space so he had to tread carefully to the seat he was offered. A glass of sparkling juice, described as, 'almost like Champagne,' was offered and after a sip or two Phil relaxed and the day was wonderful.

When the twins had been in bed several hours and everyone sleepy and yawning Phil stood to go home and Jenny rose to get his coat and say goodbye. Phil had already thanked her family and turned to thank Jenny. Before he could speak she stood on tiptoe, put her arms around his neck and kissed him.

'It's been great having you here, Phil. I hope we can meet again soon.'

'I'd really like that and thank you for inviting me it's been brilliant, even without alcohol.' He kissed her back and went out of the door feeling as if he was floating with happiness.

Two weeks later Phil arrived at Harrogate Crematorium, in a deluge of rain. Black umbrellas bumped as people met and quietly greeted each other. Jenny was already there and he went over to stand next to her, needing the support of a friend.

'May I suggest we all go inside, out of this storm,' said the funeral director and people entered the warmth of the chapel, gratefully. Jason did not move, waiting for the hearse to arrive. He wanted to be with her as she was brought in.

The coffin was unloaded onto a gurney and moved smoothly down the aisle with Jason following, blinded by tears mingled with raindrops. He didn't notice the beautiful flowers on the altar, the family and close friends or the kindly vicar waiting. An usher showed him where to sit and he did so like an automaton.

This can't be happening, he thought. It's a nightmare. My Catherine can't be dead and in that box. We had so many plans, our wish list of holidays, starting a family. Gone, it's all gone.

His desolation weighed heavy. His head drooped and shoulders hunched as the service went on, in front of him, without him.

Someone touched his arm. 'It's time to go Jason.' He barely registered the vicar but stood and moved slowly towards the dull light and the cold air. People hugged him, murmured their sadness, 'She was so lovely,' 'Too young to have died,' 'So sorry for your loss.' They didn't linger long, looking at the wreaths on the ground but walked quickly to the warmth of their cars, keen to have lunch and a happier atmosphere. He stood bleakly as they left. Dad stood beside him and then said they ought to go to the wake.

'I don't want to see everyone cheerful and glad it's all over, Dad. It will never be over for me, you or Catherine's mum and dad.'

'I know it takes time but we coped when your mum died, didn't we? The pain of losing her is less now, isn't it?'

'Yes but I'd have done anything to have Mum here now.'

'Me too.' Dad sniffed and passed Jason a clean handkerchief. Come on, you must show your face.' They got into the car and were soon at the hotel.

It was a bland room all stainless steel, glass table tops and black leather upholstery. A finger buffet was laid on a long table, lots of savouries and some small, iced cakes. The atmosphere was muted but as the wine flowed it got louder and then someone laughed. Jason clutched his glass, untouched, and followed Dad as he mingled and thanked everyone for coming. It was too hard to talk, so Jason was mute, just nodding, occasionally.

When it was finally over Dad drove him home and offered to stay with him and sleep the night.

'No. It's OK, Dad. I've got to manage on my own and I might as well start now. Thank you for helping me today and everything you've done for me since…'

It was impossible to finish the sentence. He unlocked the front door, closed it and sank to the floor sobbing.

Chapter 4

July 2016

Jason dragged himself up the stairs, exhausted but unwilling to attempt sleep, which constantly eluded him. He went lethargically through the undressing, teeth cleaning, pill popping routine and then slipped between the sheets. They were cool but soon he warmed, snuggled and shut his eyes. Since Catherine's death he had become an insomniac. The room was too quiet, the bed too big and empty but tonight he drifted away quickly and began to dream…. or was it a nightmare?

The alleyway was dark and smelled of urine, litter squelched underfoot and a woman's scream set him trembling with fear. A man shouted something and as Jason turned to see what had happened the glimmer of a streetlight suddenly disappeared blotted out by a figure running towards him.

Pounding closer the footsteps echoed and Jason's pulse raced as he pressed himself up against the damp wall. Something wet flapped against his face. He stood, paralysed until the man left and the dull glow from the light was revealed. Sighing with relief, he ventured after the man. Jason's feet made no sound as he ran to the end of the alleyway. He looked, cautiously, both ways and saw the man running downhill towards the Royal Baths, his coat tails bobbing and his white scarf streaming out behind him.

Jason awoke, instantly alert. He had been asleep barely an hour. His heart seemed to be beating abnormally fast and the details of his dream were vivid. Throwing back the duvet he went to the bathroom and put the light on, above the shaving mirror, to find his sleeping pills in the cabinet. The sight of his reflected face was shocking. It was spattered with blood! Peering closer, looking for a wound, he realised he had no pain and no cut. It was not his blood. He checked the rest of his body and saw that his feet were filthy.

No wonder I made no noise running down the alley. I had bare feet, he thought. He sat down quickly on the toilet seat feeling unsteady. His heart was racing, with the onset of an anxiety attack and he fought to calm himself. He recognised the fear and knew how to combat the rising feeling of panic and then nausea, which gradually abated.

He stripped off his nightclothes, had a shower, and then clad in his dressing gown, he returned to the bedroom. The pillowcase was smeared with blood and he felt a wave of shock threatening his stomach again. He yanked off the offending bedding and went back to the bathroom to deposit them in the washing bin, along with his nightclothes. He would have to soak them in cold water tomorrow.

How he longed to talk to Catherine. She'd been a good listener, reassuringly sensible, full of ideas and bursting with life. He missed her so much he ached but now he pushed away the threat of maudlin thoughts that inevitably led to tears. It had been six months and he had to try to make a life without her.

The dream of the alley came back into his mind. I witnessed a crime but how did I see it? Did I walk in my sleep? Did I unlock the door? I shouldn't wash the blood out. It's evidence of a crime. Perhaps forensics would want them to do some tests. I don't remember seeing a weapon and who and where was the victim?

He went downstairs and tried the front door, back and patio doors but they were all locked. It then occurred to him that filthy feet would leave marks on the wooden floor so he crawled in the most likely areas but they were all clean.

No footprints, all the doors locked, so how did it happen?

He made a cup of tea and took it into his den; Catherine had called it that. The computer sat on a large mahogany desk, bookshelves from floor to ceiling on two walls and under the window was the glass-fronted cabinet containing what she termed his 'nautical nonsense.' He looked at the ship's timer, gleaming after his efforts to clean it the day before.

The opposite corner of the room housed a large leather armchair that would have graced a gentleman's club, in a previous era. He curled up in it now and thought about the crime he had heard and wondered at the mysterious circumstances. He wanted to know more. He could go back to the alley in the morning and see if he could find any evidence but it was likely the police had already got it under control.

Jason began to feel drowsy, the sleeping pill taking effect, so he returned to the bedroom. The bed had no sheet. He hesitated then lay down on the bare mattress and pulled the duvet over himself. His last thought, brought a rueful smile to his face, was what Catherine would think of him sleeping in an unmade bed?

Brilliant sunlight streamed through a chink in the curtains and woke him. He stretched, relishing the slow start to a Sunday and then remembered the dream and leapt out of bed. He dressed in tracksuit and trainers, had a cup of tea and went for a run. Before Catherine died he had run every morning before breakfast but depression had brought lethargy and he had not felt any desire to do it, until today.

He ran steadily but his lack of fitness meant he had to stop to allow his breathing to slow, several times. He used to run the same route, about three miles, but on weekends he varied it and today he found himself pounding towards the place he'd recognised the night before. When he reached the top of the hill, he slowed to a walk and continued down until he reached the end of the alley. As he walked along it everything seemed wider and much cleaner than in his dream.

Perhaps it looks different because it's a lovely sunny day, he thought. He continued until it opened out into a junction. Was this the scene of the crime? He looked closely at the pavement, searching for any sign of blood but there was nothing. He shrugged feeling a little disappointed and set off to run back home.

It was still early so he made himself some breakfast and took it into the den. He sat at his desk and picked up the phone.

Phil answered sleepily, 'What time do you call this on a Sunday morning?'

'I've been for a run and wondered, if you could possibly drag yourself out of bed, if you fancied a sail?'

'Great, but we'll have missed the first race by the time we get there and rigged the boat. Are you sure you're ready?'

'Yes. I feel much more positive today and it's time I faced people. Anyway it's a gorgeous day and at least force four.'

'Right I'll pick you up in about half an hour.'

When they got to the sailing lake most people were on the water engaged in the first race. They smiled or waved their recognition of his return, after Catherine's death, so there were no embarrassing moments with people wanting to say they were sorry but not wanting to hurt him.

They rigged the *Enterprise*. The familiar clanging of stays on metal masts and the flapping as the sails were pulled up delighted Jason. 'It's ages since I've done this - hope I haven't lost my touch.'

'Sailing's like riding a bike,' said Phil. 'Come on let's get her down the slipway.'

They entered two races and came second both times.

'Do you think we're carrying too much weight?' asked Phil, smoothing his middle aged paunch ruefully.

'Probably,' said Jason, looking at the young, lithe figures of the crew that had beaten them. 'But I must admit I really enjoyed making them work hard for their triumph.' He laughed and then stopped abruptly, guilty to have laughed; guilty he had enjoyed his day, with Catherine so recently gone. Phil put his hand on his shoulder and whispered, 'She loved you, Jason, and she wouldn't want you to sit and mourn forever. What would you like to do now? I can take you home or we could have a bite at the Golden Lion. The choice is yours.' Jason was hungry and realised he had spent a long time feeling numb.

'Let's go to the pub. I fancy a meat pie with loads of gravy, but before that I must go and speak to Sean. Emily must be expecting her baby any day and I want to ask how she is. Sean was just pulling the cover over his boat and turned with a smile when Jason called his name. He held out his hand. 'It's good to see you back sailing again, Jason. You and Phil did well after such a long break.'

'It felt great to be back on the water but I really came to ask after Emily. She would normally crew for you and I wondered if she'd had the baby?'

'Thanks for thinking of us. She hasn't had it, sorry, him, yet but is huge and suffering from backache. She can't wait to go into labour and it shouldn't be long. Her due date is two weeks today. This will be my last sail for a while because I don't want to leave her when it's so close.'

'Will you tell her I asked? And good luck with everything that's to come.' Sean smiled and nodded as Jason left him to re-join Phil.

Later, sitting back full of pie and beer Jason said, 'We've been friends for quite a while, since Uni What would that be, ten years?' Phil nodded. Jason wanted to tell him about his bizarre dream but realised Phil would think him crazy. 'I want to presume on our friendship but I'm not sure if I should.'

'You'll never know if you don't ask so, fire away.'

'If I gave you a piece of cloth with a bloodstain would it be possible for you to analyse it for me, DNA and all that?' He saw Phil frown. 'Sorry. I shouldn't have asked.'

'Just a minute, you ask me something really odd and then back off. What's this all about?'

'Nothing much, just curious, sorry.'

'I'll think about it while we drive home. Come on.'

When they got back Jason invited Phil in. He hesitated saying he had some chores to do, but Jason said, 'I won't keep you five minutes. I just want to show you my latest acquisition. You'll like it. I bought it just before Catherine died and I've been so unsociable I'd not thought of showing it to you, until today.'

Phil nodded and joined Jason in the den. They went across to the cabinet and Phil whistled. 'That's a beautiful ship's timer. Is it genuine?'

'It's got *Daphne* engraved on the base so I think it is.'

He opened the cabinet door and handed Phil the timer. He looked at the base, and turned it upside down, watching the sand fall.

24

'It's lovely, heavy too with all that brass.' He handed it back to Jason who returned it to the cabinet.

As they went together to the front door Phil said, 'You asked me to do an analysis. Well I think it might be possible but it'll cost you.'

'How much?'

Phil grinned, 'A race again next week and you buy the meal.'

'Wow, thanks Phil I'll go and fetch it.' He ran upstairs, retrieved the pillowcase and ran down with it in his hand.

'Can you cut out the bit with the blood so it's a smaller size for me to smuggle in to the lab? You should put it into a small bag too.' When Jason returned Phil pocketed the sample and went home.

Later that evening, feeling physically tired after the fresh air and exercise, Jason was confident he would sleep well and he did, to begin with. But then he found himself in the same dark alley.

The scream made his heart beat faster but there was no paralysing fear this time. He waited for the footsteps to pound away from him but did not go in pursuit. He turned instead towards the sound of the scream.

A woman was lying on the pavement, her head cranked awkwardly against a wall. Black looking blood was seeping through her hair and pooling like a halo. Jason knelt down and felt for her pulse. 'Hello. Can you hear me? My name's Jason and I'm going to help you.'

There was no response and no pulse. He looked around to see if there was anyone else who could help but it was late and the street was empty. He took off his top, used it as a bandage and then gently slid her down to make her more comfortable. After several minutes of compressions and mouth to mouth he was sweating with the exertion but pushed himself to continue, hoping for a miracle.

'Hey! Police! What are you up to?'

This was followed by a piercing whistle, the sound of boots pounding towards him…. and Jason woke up.

He was in bed but threw off the duvet and rushed to the bathroom. This time he was not surprised to see his bare torso and bloody hands. He rested his forehead against the cold mirror. What was happening? Recurring dream? How could it be when evidence of it was all over him? He needed another shower.

The hot water was soothing. It ran pink off his hands as he scrubbed them. He turned so it ran down his back allowing the warmth to pour over him long after he was clean.

When he was dry and wrapped in his dressing gown he repeated the previous night's routine taking a cup of tea into the den. Now, as he settled into his chair, he allowed himself to think about the dream.

The woman was slim with a straight, sleeveless dress flaring out with little pleats at the bottom. It was pale blue or lilac, and her shoes had a bow of the same shade. Her hair was light, fair or possibly auburn and short around a mature but beautiful, oval face. He thought she would be in her mid thirties. She had a soft evening bag lying beside her. The 1920s came to mind. The man who ran by him was wearing a tailcoat. Must have been a fancy dress do. Should have looked in her bag, found out who she was, he thought.

He sipped his tea and grimaced. He hated cold tea. Then he realised he must have been thinking for quite a while.

There was something wrong with the scene of the crime. He focused less now on the woman and tried to see the surrounding street. It was so dingy as if several streetlights were out. He sat up straight as he realised they were gas lamps.

She wasn't in costume. He'd gone back in time.

How could this happen? Surely it was impossible. Things like this only happened in sci-fi films or fantasy. He felt out of his depth and needed to talk about it.

Immediately Sonia came to mind. In the morning he would ring her and see if she would have lunch with him. She would listen, without laughing at him.

Sonia had always been Catherine's friend but when Jason arrived he was immediately accepted too. She was a little older than them but a delight to be with. The reason he had thought of her as a confidante was her inability to be shocked. For Sonia life was full of wonder and anything was possible. He had neglected to keep in touch since the funeral but knew she would understand.

Having made that decision he felt better, returned to bed and slept soundly, without dreaming, until the alarm woke him.

26

Jason got ready for work, ate some cereal and decided to do a load of washing. There were now two sets of soiled bedding, after all. He dragged the bin to the machine, stuffed the sheets into it and then stopped. Was there a cold soak programme? There was, so he left it to do its job, and went to school.

When he arrived everyone was anxious because an OFSTED team were coming, with no prior warning, to do an inspection. Jason ran through his timetable in his mind and felt reasonably confident. It was getting close to Sports Day so every class he had was doing athletics. He set the field out, with the help of Jenny who did P.E. part-time, but was with him that morning. When his first class was changed it was all organised and under control. The sun came out and his heart rose as he realised he was coping with the situation so well. Just a few weeks ago a visit from OFSTED would have found him off sick with stress. Something had happened to give him a zest for life again and he revelled in it.

His new bout of energy and enthusiasm showed as he ran from group to group encouraging and helping, while an inspector watched. Jason knew he had done well by the end of the day and went home feeling pleased. The inspection would continue tomorrow but his department was done so he could relax.

That evening he felt the familiar oppression of the empty house and then remembered he had intended to phone Sonia. The whole OFSTED thing had put it right out of his mind. He put the kettle on, found some biscuits and then rang her.

'Sonia? It's Jason.'

'Hello stranger, it's been a while.'

'Yes I know but I wasn't in a good place and couldn't socialise with anyone.'

'I did know that but you sound quite positive at the moment. Were you just phoning for a chat or was there something specific?'

'I was hoping we could meet for lunch on Saturday. Are you free?'

When Jason put the phone down it was all arranged. He wondered what she would think of his weird experiences and hoped she would reassure him, somehow.

Chapter 5

Harrogate July 1929

Captain David Morris cursed as he yanked the bow tie undone.

'Why can I never tie these damn things right the first time?'

There was no reply because he was alone, getting dressed to go to a ball at The Majestic Hotel. Finally, satisfied with his tie, he smoothed his slightly greying hair and lit up a cigar. He was early now so he would sit and enjoy a smoke before setting out. David settled into his winged chair and anticipated the evening ahead.

Annabelle, a beautiful and wealthy widow he had been pursuing for some months, would be there. He was not the only man showing interest in her but at the moment he thought she favoured him and he might, if she gave him the chance, try popping the question this evening.

He needed her money to get rid of his debts and to help him live the lifestyle of an officer and a gentleman. Did he love her? Well he felt sure he could bed her and he did find her amusing. He stood up muttering, 'She'll do. Annabelle Larkin, here I come.'

David strode down the road - no money to waste on a cab - but it was a beautiful warm evening and he was happy to walk. As he swung along it was easy to see he had been a military man. His head was up, his shoulders back and he carried a cane tucked under his arm. He had been a civilian for fourteen years but old habits were hard to break.

As the imposing hotel came into view, he paused. It was a huge brick building, the centre of the roofline topped with a dome. Carriages were arriving and a few cars. How he wished he could arrive in style and whisk her off her feet. It was an ideal setting to woo her.

Wasting no more time he entered, feeling excited and alive. After divesting himself of the cane and white scarf, he gazed around the foyer hoping to spot a friend or Annabelle herself. She was not obvious but he saw Caruthers, a comrade in arms, so David threaded his way through the crowd to chat to him.

'Good to see you, old chap. I'm badly in need of a drink. Join me?'

Caruthers nodded and they squeezed their way to the bar.

'Beer? Whisky?' asked David, hoping he would opt for beer.

'Beer please, this warm weather gives a man a thirst.'

David grinned, ordered two beers which they drank standing with their backs to the bar, surveying the throng.

'You seen much of the merry widow?' asked Caruthers.

'I'm hoping to see her tonight. She said she was coming when I saw her at Mary Guest's soiree.'

'Oh. I wasn't invited to that, probably because I was a lieutenant. Don't quite make the grade.'

'Nonsense the war was years ago. We're more enlightened now, surely. The music's getting livelier, making my feet tap. Shall we move to the ballroom?'

'I think I'll wait here a little longer, not really a dancer; might meet up with Captain Henderson.'

That was not good news to David. Captain Henderson was his rival for Annabelle's affections. He walked towards the ballroom hoping Caruthers would keep Henderson thoroughly occupied.

Pausing at the entrance to the ballroom he scarcely saw the ornate swathed windows, the glittering chandeliers and elegant columns. He scanned the people, ignoring the evening suited men, searching the dazzling array of beautiful, wealthy women dancing or sipping drinks at the tables. There she was. Annabelle was sitting, chatting with some animation, to an elderly couple, possibly her parents. He edged towards her and finally arrived just as the band struck up a Charleston.

He smiled down at her. She looked beautiful in a powder blue dress that showed her slim figure to perfection. 'Mrs Larkin, delighted to see you here this evening.' He looked enquiringly at her companions. 'I don't think I've had the pleasure?'

'No you haven't,' said Annabelle. 'This is my aunt and uncle, Mr and Mrs Anderson.' She turned towards them, and as they shook hands she said, 'I'd like you to meet my friend, Captain Morris.'

'Pleased to meet you, Captain. Would you like to join us? There's plenty of room,' said Mr Harrison.'

'Thank you I'd be delighted. But first I can't resist a Charleston so would you join me Annabelle?' She grinned happily, stood up and he led her formally by the hand onto the dance floor. Then all formality ceased as they abandoned themselves to the jittering gyrations necessary to execute the dance. When it was finished they were breathless, flushed and happy. David led her back to her seat but stayed standing as she sat.

'Would you like me to get some drinks?' he offered, hoping they would refuse.

'No thank you we've barely started these. Not sure about Annabelle, though. She seems to have finished her's already.' His tone seemed to suggest disapproval but she was not fazed.

'Champagne for me please, it's so refreshingly decadent.' She smiled wickedly up at him and David's heart lurched, despite the expense.

He set off for the bar but grimaced as he approached seeing Henderson talking to Caruthers. His hands showed he was relating a story and, by the violence of the moves, probably a war time one. Most soldiers who survived in 1918 rarely spoke about the deprivation, fear and horror they had endured. But there were exceptions and Henderson was one who loved to brag. David suspected he had enjoyed a quiet war, possibly in admin or something and made up tales to impress.

In some ways David had had a relatively easy war himself, being in communications with the 18th Battalion, 1st Tyneside Pioneers. He'd never had to stand in a trench awaiting an order to advance over the top. It was his job, either on foot, or horseback to bring those orders. The sight of the dead and the screams of the injured still haunted him at night but he never talked about it. That was all behind him now and his penury was a much more pressing problem.

'Evening Henderson,' he said as he arrived at the bar, hoping one of them would offer to buy and he was not disappointed. Caruthers was genial enough, even adding a 'glass of bubbly for the little lady' too.

'So what about Wilfred Rhodes then, one thousand cricket matches, eh?' said David.

'He's probably the best cricketer ever,' said Henderson. 'I saw him play once in Leeds. He was superb. Makes you proud to think he's a Yorkshire lad like us.'

The bar tender brought the drinks and David continued to chat for a few minutes, drinking the top off his beer before excusing himself. 'Thanks, old man for the drinks; nice seeing you Henderson, must go, can't let Annabelle die of thirst.' His words were uttered with a smile of triumph, knowing Henderson would be discomforted by the mention of the 'little lady's' name.

There was a hint of a swagger as he made his way through the thinning crowd near the bar and entered the frenzied atmosphere of the ballroom. He carefully negotiated the flailing arms and legs and arrived at Annabelle's table without mishap. He put down the drinks and invited her onto the dance floor again. She stood up, had a quick sip of her champagne and they joined the throng.

At the end of the dance he suggested they went into the garden for some fresh air and she happily agreed. They strolled, contentedly discussing the merits of balls at the Majestic and tea dances at the Royal Hall.

'I think evening dances are far more romantic than those in the afternoon,' David ventured.

'Really?' she giggled. 'I thought it was only girls who filled their heads with silly romantic thoughts.'

'Not so,' David smiled. 'What man would not envy me now walking through the rose garden with a beautiful woman on my arm?'

She snuggled closer at the compliment, looked shyly up at him and he stole a kiss –just a gentle brush of the lips. He was anxious not to frighten her by a display of passion. She looked to see if any other people were around, then seeing they were alone, she pulled him closer and kissed him in a way no decent woman should. He was on fire and considered pushing her down onto the lawn to see just how keen she was but something held him back.

'You're a tease.' He grinned and hugged her, knowing any sudden moves could be his undoing. This woman was worth waiting for.

They returned to the dance floor in time for the last waltz, which they did in style. David confidently steered and controlled her every move and knew they looked good together. They returned to their table, after applauding the band, to finish their drinks. Mr and Mrs Anderson smiled as they approached but not with their eyes.

'Have you been in the garden?' asked Mrs Anderson. 'I believe the roses are beautiful and smell heavenly.'

Annabelle blushed and nodded. 'Yes the roses were beautiful and it was positively crowded in the garden. It's such a warm evening.'

'While you were taking the air I ordered a cab,' said Mr Anderson. 'You could join us. We'd be happy to drop you wherever you live Captain Morris.'

'Thank you so much but we couldn't trouble you,' Annabelle said. 'It's late and you have a long journey to Birstwith. I'm sure Captain Morris will see me safely home,' turning to him for confirmation.

'It would be my pleasure,' he agreed truthfully, hardly able to believe his luck.

When the Andersons left they sat again, sipped their drinks and talked. It was easier without the chaperones and the noise of the band. They were comfortable together and David wondered if he was falling in love. Eventually there were so few people left in the ballroom they felt obliged to move towards the exit. David collected her stole and his silk scarf and cane from the hatcheck girl and when they emerged into the warm evening there were no cabs left.

'Oh what rotten luck.' said David, 'We'll have to wait. I'm sure one will come soon, unless you would like to walk?' He willed her to agree.

'Why not? – It's less than a mile and I'm not in the least bit tired.'

He smiled, gave her his arm and they walked in easy silence for a while. David was anxious to broach the subject of marriage but not sure when or how to begin.

'I've really enjoyed this evening,' she said. 'I just love dancing, don't you? You cut quite a figure in the Charleston.'

'Thank you but dancing is no fun unless you have a beautiful, talented partner, like you.' His arm left hers and crept around her waist and there was no resistance. They walked slowly talking about future dances and dinners until they reached the end of her street.

He had to ask her now. 'I think you know, Annabelle, that I find you devilish attractive. I felt tonight we were the perfect couple and ….'

'Hush,' she interrupted. 'I don't want you to go any further David. Don't spoil things, please.'

'I don't want to spoil anything but I want to tell you how I feel. Don't you feel anything for me?'

She turned to face him. 'You're fun to be with and I do like you a lot but I'm frightened of committing myself to a relationship. When Archie died in the war I was devastated, completely lost. It's hard to let myself fall in love and risk feeling that pain again.'

'Oh Annabelle, I'd never hurt you. The war is long over. Many people lost their loved ones but life goes on. Please think about it. You see I've fallen for you completely, utterly. Don't make me say hopelessly.'

David felt desperate to press his case, suddenly realising that his need for her went well beyond his need for her money. His arms went out to pull her towards him when she screamed. He turned just in time to receive a mighty blow from a cudgel that should have killed him but it glanced across the side of his head then his shoulder. Annabelle received the follow-through that knocked her to the ground. He staggered but kept on his feet, wavering and the thief took the opportunity to take his watch, his silver topped cane and the few coins he had left. Annabelle's purse was lying on the floor but that was hard to reach with David quickly coming to his senses.

The thief ran fast, down an alley, while David hovered with uncertainty. 'Annabelle, Annabelle!' He didn't know what to do. He bent down, shook her shoulder but she seemed to be unconscious. Suddenly he was fired with anger and followed the thief, staggering as he tried to run down the alley.

Chapter 6

2016

Sonia was of medium build, had medium brown hair and was approaching middle age but that is where the Mrs Average ended. Being with Sonia was soothing, like snuggling under a thick duvet. Her smile was alight with intelligence, humour and kindliness. She had a ready wit, but never made other people the butt of it and she was a superb listener.

She dressed with elegance in long, flowing skirts and delighted in beads and bangles. All this was teamed with expensive boots in the winter or simple sandals in the summer.

Sonia, now a widow, had private means. Several years ago she resigned from her teaching career and now travelled and studied as the whim took her. She had an enquiring mind that was interested in everything from the smallest bug to space travel.

Now she paused at the door of Betty's Tea Room, scanned the hive of activity then smiled as she saw Jason waving and rising to greet her. She noticed he was thinner, his dark hair needed cutting and he had that blue beard look that was so popular on television. He looked handsome, particularly now that he was grinning; a lovely welcome. She wiggled her way between the close-knit tables her baggy, diaphanous sleeves threatening to sweep cakes off elegant stands but she arrived without mishap and they embraced delightedly.

'It really is lovely to see you. You look so well too, if just a little thin,' she said. Jason agreed he was generally feeling better and both avoided mentioning that the last time they'd met had been Catherine's funeral.

'Now, as I'm sure you've been neglecting to cook, this is my treat and you should indulge yourself.'

'You don't have to treat me,' he objected, half-heartedly. He knew it would be pointless.

'Yes I do. I've missed you just as much as I've missed Catherine,' she said, ignoring his wince at the mention of her name.

'And this is my way of welcoming you back as a very special friend.' She paused, sighed and then said brightly. 'Right that's enough sentimentality, let's order.'

They were silent as they perused the menu and looked up simultaneously having chosen. Jason gave the order to the waitress, a salmon salad with a glass of Chardonnay for Sonia, fish and chips for himself with a glass of lager.

When the waitress had gone she became serious and said, 'I have a feeling this meeting is not just because you wanted to see me again. I feel you have an ulterior motive and whatever it is, I'll try to help.' She stretched her hand across the table and took his.

'This is one of the things I love about you, Sonia; I swear you have some kind of sixth sense.' Encouraged by her smile he pressed on, anxious to share his dreams. 'It is that special sixth sense of yours that I need. I have had a couple of very unusual and frightening dreams.'

He told her everything, watching her face for incredulity or frank disbelief but her face just showed interest. He finished with, 'Then I woke up and there was blood all over my hands from a deep gash on her forehead.'

Sonia had sat motionless but just as she was about to speak their meal arrived. Neither began to eat.

'This is quite a bizarre tale and if anyone less level headed than you had told me I would think it was fiction. Anything is possible but supernatural phenomena like this are very rare. I think you are possibly being haunted.'

'Well that's a relief; I thought you would tell me to consult a shrink! I feel so much better just by telling you. In fact I can do justice to this lunch now.'

He picked up his knife and fork and ate with enthusiasm. She ate with less appetite, deep in thought, saying nothing. When his plate was empty he sighed with satisfaction, picked up his beer and drank deeply.

Sonia left the rest of her meal and, wine glass in hand, said, 'I think we should meet again soon, when I have had time to think about all this properly. Could I visit you next weekend?'

Jason nodded, 'Saturday, any time, not Sunday, because I've just taken up sailing again.'

'Have you? I'm really pleased you're picking up your life again. Saturday will be fine. What about making me coffee about eleven?'

They parted with a light kiss at Bettys' door and Jason went back to his car with the intention of going to a supermarket. He stopped when his mobile rang and saw it was Phil.

'I hope you're ready for this, Jason. I found a filial match to that sample you gave me and the man's in prison!'

'Wow. What's his name? What did he do?'

'He's called Nathan Morris and his DNA was on file because he's currently serving time in Armley Gaol. I did a bit of digging and it seems he's close to finishing a two-year stretch, having served nine months, for a spate of robberies. So, are you going to explain what this is all about?'

Jason hesitated. What could he say? Finally he said, 'Sorry Phil. I'm grateful for the information and I'll buy you a massive dinner tomorrow. But I'd prefer to keep this to myself for the moment.'

Phil took it well. They exchanged knowledge about the predicted wind force and made arrangements for meeting the next day.

Jason reached his car and sat in it without moving for a few minutes, thinking. Perhaps he could visit this Nathan Morris and have a chat about his, father. No it would have to be his grandfather. Jason started the engine and as he drove to the supermarket he thought how exciting it was to have a possible lead to his mysterious dreams.

The shop was crowded and he started to walk through the fruit and veg to the packet meals and then stopped. Catherine produced all meals from fresh ingredients and this new man inside him wanted to be healthier. He bought strawberries, bananas, stir-fry vegetables, potatoes and two chicken breasts. A few more necessities went into the trolley and he was through the check–out and back in his car within twenty minutes.

At home Jason put away his groceries and made a mug of tea. He took it into his den and sat down at the computer. He put into Google, 'murders of women in Yorkshire in the 1920s'. This seemed to give him female murderers and when he changed the search to 'unsolved murders' it seemed to think people were only interested in

London. He also tried 'Nathan Morris' and discovered there was a popular young evangelical pastor by that name but he was unlikely to be a relative of a felon in a gaol in Leeds.

It was difficult to think of anything else at the moment so he decided to see if he could talk to Nathan. He had no idea if he would be allowed to visit him but he thought of a plausible reason. He could pose as a writer researching to find out if the criminal mind could be inherited.

That night Jason slept well, without dreaming and was almost disappointed when he woke to find it was morning and he had seen nothing to add to his information. It was quite early so he went for a run before breakfast and arrived home in time to go sailing.

Phil picked him up as before. They rigged the boat, working efficiently together and trundled it into the water for the first race of the day.

'I've got a good feeling about this, Phil. I've bought healthy food and I swear I've lost two pounds just by looking at it in the fridge.'

Phil laughed. 'I'm not sure it's you who needs to lose weight but I like your optimism. There's plenty of wind so let's go.'

They did win the first and second races and after a snack lunch they entered the final one of the day, supremely confident, and came second.

'That'll teach us to be less cocky. Just a smidgen late across the line and we couldn't make it up. Still, better than last week,' Phil said. 'All this fresh air's given me an appetite. I'm looking forward to this blow out you're going to buy me.'

Jason grinned in reply as they de-rigged the boat and pulled it to the dinghy park. Finally they carried the sails and their bags to Phil's car and set off home. They had agreed to walk to the pub so they could both have a beer and they met again in an hour, showered and tidy.

'You've caught the sun, Phil. Didn't you remember your sun screen?' He looked at the Roman, very red nose and the blue eyes, under the sore forehead.

Phil just shrugged, sweeping back a lock of fair hair with a wince.

'We can't all be, 'easy tan' men like you. And yes I did forget. I was more interested in the strength of the wind when I listened to the forecast.'

They ordered their Sunday dinner, drank their beers and Jason told Phil about the OFSTED visit. Phil knew nothing about teaching but had heard horror tales from other teacher friends and was pleased when he heard it had gone well.

'How did Jenny fare?'

'I don't know how she did in Music but in P.E. she did very well. I'm surprised she hasn't told you about it.'

'She did. She said her music lessons were well received but she hadn't had feedback on her P.E.'

'Well none of us know the final outcome yet. I'm just going by the comments given on the day.'

The dinners arrived, were consumed with enthusiasm and Phil managed apple pie and custard too, saying he intended to get his money's worth even if it made him sick.

'So you're starting your diet tomorrow?' asked Jason, his eyebrows raised with a mocking grin.

'That's totally under the belt when I'm relishing every mouthful,' said Phil as he finished the pie and sat back with a sigh. He tenderly rubbed his stomach with his hands and looked at Jason. 'Ok, I'm full to bursting and still very curious about that sample. How did you get a pillow case with some blood on it related to a man in prison?'

Jason fidgeted. 'I can't tell you the story at the moment. It's a bit of a mystery and I'm trying to solve it. I promise I'll reveal all when I have.'

'Thought you'd say that. Right we'd better go. Work tomorrow. Thanks for the meal. See you next week?'

'Yes. I've nothing else on.'

Jason walked home, organised his kit for school the next day and got ready for bed. I wonder if I'll find out more tonight? He thought. He slipped into bed but could not relax into sleep. Finally he sat up and took a sleeping pill, feeling annoyed because he was trying to wean himself off them. He knew what the problem was. He wanted to go back and see if the man that shouted would help him save the woman. There had been a whistle so he must have been a policeman. Why did the dream stop there?

At lunchtime on Monday he telephoned Armley Gaol and was told he could visit on Friday but it would have to be during working hours or Saturday morning at 9am. Visiting was limited to one hour so if he went on Saturday he could be back in time to make coffee for Sonia. He made the appointment, bought a sandwich for lunch, and returned to work.

The rest of the week went by with no dreams and on Saturday Jason wondered if it had all been his overwrought imagination but there was real, physical evidence so he decided to pursue it.

Armley Gaol looked like a castle from the front view. It was an old Victorian building but the visitors' centre had been modernised and seemed bright and as welcoming as such a place could be. It was not the depressing scene he had expected. There were several families waiting when he got there and, after security checks, they all entered a large room with the prisoners sitting at individual tables. Jason had to ask for help because he had no idea what Nathan looked like. The prison officer introduced them and Jason sat opposite a flabby middle-aged man with thinning brown hair and large bi-focal glasses perched on a hooked nose. He was not a handsome man and this impression was enhanced when he opened his mouth to smile revealing nicotine stained teeth.

'Well, Mr Brownlow is it?' Jason nodded. 'I was surprised when they told me you were coming but whatever you want I'm happy to see you. The days don't 'arf drag in 'ere and I never get no visitors. So, what's up?'

'To start with I'd like to call you Nathan, so please call me Jason. This is nothing formal.'

'Ok, Jason, fire away.'

'I'm doing some research into the criminal mind and whether it could be hereditary. It's in the early stages. You are the first person I've interviewed so forgive me if I seem a bit inefficient. He put his notepad on the table and, pen poised, said, 'Can I ask what made you begin a life of crime?'

Nathan screwed up his face as he thought how to answer. Eventually he said, slowly, 'I'm not a criminal. You've started with the wrong one, sorry.'

Jason put down his pen. 'You mean you didn't rob anyone?'

'No, well, not just mysel' like. I was egged on. I didn't want to do it. I'm not really a criminal you see. I just got in with the wrong crowd when I was young. Mam did 'er best but she had a lot on 'er 'ands with the littleuns an' Dad running off and leavin' 'er to cope.'

'What did your dad do? For a living, I mean.'

'I think he were a labourer when I was nowt but a nipper then he got injured and weren't fit. He were weak. I don't mean he was ill or anything. He just couldn't handle being out o' work, too many mouths to feed and all that. So he left us.'

'Did he survive by stealing or do anything criminal?'

Nathan shifted in his seat. 'Not that I know of. Mam didn't talk about him much.'

Jason made a rueful face. 'It seems my idea of inheriting a criminal streak could be wrong.' He closed his notepad and put his pen in his pocket, preparing to go.

'Just wait a sec,' said Nathan, enjoying himself. 'You asked about me dad. You didn't ask nothin' about me grandpa. You see *he* was a convicted murderer. He was hanged, here in this very gaol.'

'Really? Who did he kill?'

'He murdered an heiress.'

'When was that?'

'Oh, I don't know, sometime in the late 1920s, early 30s. Couldn't give exact figures. I know me dad never knew him 'cause he was just a baby.'

'What was your grandfather's first name?'

'No idea but he was an officer in the First World War. There wasn't much around that belonged to my grandpa but somewhere at 'ome, I've got 'is pocket watch. It's a real nice piece and several times I've thought of selling it but never did.'

'Fantastic! Thanks Nathan. I'll have to go in a minute; just one more question. Are you married and have you any children?'

'No. I've got sense, I have. Right early on I decided I wouldn't have the burden round my neck of wife and kids to support. Good job really when you look at me now. What about you? I bet you've got all the works, nice house, pretty wife and at least two kids.'

Jason stood to go and held out his hand as he answered. 'I have a house, but no wife or kids.'

A bell rang to signal the end of the visiting time.

'I really have to go now. Thank you for talking to me. Could I come again if I need any more help?' Nathan nodded. 'I could probably suggest other people in here that you could talk to. My cellmate's always boasting about what his Dad got up to and got away with.'

They shook hands and Jason walked to the door where he turned and looked back to wave. He watched Nathan's back as he shuffled towards the prisoner's exit. He looked a lonely, pathetic man and Jason felt sorry for him.

The fresh, warm air outside revived his spirits and he went home eagerly to put the coffee pot on for Sonia's visit. He had a lot to tell her.

Chapter 7

Harrogate 1929

David stopped running, his chest heaving for breath and feeling light headed. He bent forwards, supporting himself with his hands on his knees. He waited until his breathing became less laboured then stood carefully upright. A wave of pain coursed through his head. The assailant had run too fast. He was unable to catch him. David turned to go back to Annabelle. She would think he'd deserted her. He staggered back up the hill and eventually entered the dark alley.

As he emerged into the lighter area, where they had been attacked, he stopped. There was a hearse. A doctor and policemen surrounded Annabelle. David stood, paralysed by shock, watching as they lifted her body gently onto a stretcher and then into the hearse. They'd covered her face. She was dead. It was like watching a silent film and then he realised that people were talking quietly but he couldn't hear what they were saying. The blow to his head must have made him deaf in one ear. He put his hand up to his head and it came away sticky with congealing blood.

What should he do? Should he go to them and say what had happened? His legs refused to move and the hearse drove away. The doctor picked up his bag and shook hands with the policeman in charge before leaving. David watched it all until the scene before him was totally empty of people and then he leant against the wall and cried.

When his sobbing had reduced to shuddering breaths, David began to walk, aimlessly. The sky was lightening, so it must have been about four o'clock when he found himself outside a familiar house. It belonged to Caruthers. He felt exhausted and desperate for a kind word so he struggled up the steps and rang the bell. There was no answer so he rang again and saw a light come on in the entrance hall. There was a sound of bolts being drawn and then the door swung open. Caruthers stood there in his dressing gown.

'Oh. …Captain Morris, er ..David. …Sorry, come in, old boy, you look terrible. Sit down and I'll .. er fetch some cloths, bandages.

What happened? Sorry, let's get you cleaned up and see what the damage is.'

'Thank you, I'm sorry to intrude like this. I know it's very late but I didn't know who else to turn to.'

'Don't worry about that, old boy. Come and sit down and I'll clean up your head. Dear oh dear you've had a heavy blow, probably should have a stitch or two. I'll put a thick pad on it and bandage it.'

Caruthers found his medical skills, honed in the war, had not left him and David was soon sporting a white turban.

'There. You look a bit better now but I can't say the same for your evening suit. Blood is the very devil to remove. I'll fix you a drink, brandy I think for both of us and then you can tell me what happened.'

'Thank you, my ear's throbbing. Is it all still there? How can I be thinking how I'll look when,....when Annabelle's dead.'

'Dead?' Caruthers paused in his pouring of drinks, a decanter hovering in his hand. He put it down. 'David how can Annabelle be dead? We were all at the ball just a few hours ago. What the devil's happened?'

'I offered to take her home. There were no cabs so we walked. We stopped and I had just asked her to marry me.' Tears streamed down his face and he brushed them away angrily. 'She was looking up at me and she screamed as a thief heaved a club at my head. I turned and he caught the side of my head and my ear but it hit Annabelle full on her forehead. We both fell but I managed to stagger up. I called and called Annabelle but she was unconscious and there was a lot of blood. It was that same feeling we got in the war when a mate was killed. You just wanted revenge, so I ran after him.'

Caruthers nodded, with understanding. 'So did you catch him?'

David shook his head and told him the rest of the story finishing with, 'I don't know what to do.'

Caruthers placed a glass of brandy on the table next to David. He put his hand on his friend's shoulder and squeezed it in sympathy. 'I don't know the answer but whatever you do it must wait until morning. You are too exhausted to cope with any more tonight, so I suggest you finish your drink and use my spare bed.'

They drank in silence, both thinking of that beautiful, vivacious woman; struggling to believe she was dead.

When he retired for what was left of the night Caruthers found it impossible to sleep. He kept re-living the horror of seeing his friend covered in blood on his doorstep and his horrific story. David had been so happy just a few hours before and he had proposed to her just as they were attacked. With a sigh he gave up the struggle and got up. He knew his housekeeper would be arriving soon so he dressed and waited for her.

Mary arrived and let herself in, quietly as usual. She was surprised to see Caruthers dressed but he quickly told her about his guest and asked her to make breakfast for two. She took a tray up to David and, about an hour later, he arrived downstairs, in borrowed clothes, looking pale and ill.

'Did you get any sleep? I didn't,' said Caruthers.

'I was exhausted and, despite the pain in my head, I did sleep. The brandy helped. Thank you for last night and the clean clothes. I've decided to go to the police station this morning.'

'Good. I'm sure that's the right thing to do. I'll come with you.'

'There's no need. You've done so much for me already. I owe it to Annabelle to help track down her killer.'

David left the house and walked to the police station. His head was throbbing and he still felt weak with shock. He entered the door and announced who he was to the duty sergeant.

'Ah, Captain Morris, Detective Peterson was going to visit you this morning. Seems you have saved us the trouble. I'll tell him you're here. Please take a seat while you're waiting.' David wanted to say, with haughty dignity, he preferred to stand but he needed to sit and went to a long bench.

He waited just a few minutes and then a slim, young man with piercing blue eyes came to him with his hand outstretched.

'I'm Detective Peterson, Captain Morris. Would you come with me so we can talk in private.'

David stood up and followed him into a small, bare office. There was just a table and two chairs and he sat in the one held for him.

Peterson then moved to the other and drew some notepaper towards him.

'Now perhaps you can tell me what happened last night after you left the ball with Mrs Larkin.'

'How do you know I was with her?'

'Mrs Larkin's purse held a ticket to the ball so we made enquiries during the night and you were seen leaving the Majestic Hotel together.'

David told his story ending with his overnight stay with Caruthers.

'Well that explains why we couldn't find you at your flat.'

'You've been looking for me?'

'We needed to talk to you because you were the last person to be seen with Mrs Larkin and, therefore, our prime suspect for her murder.'

'You can't think I murdered Annabelle. I loved her. I told you I had just asked her to marry me.'

'Calm down sir, you've made it quite clear that you were both attacked and your head wound indicates you were telling the truth. We have your description of the attacker and will be looking for him. Please stay in town because I may want to talk to you again.' He stood up. 'Thank you for coming.'

He accompanied David to the door and watched him descend the steps before turning back into the station.

The sergeant at the desk spoke. 'So what do you think? Is he a suspect?'

'Everyone's a suspect until we solve the crime, George. His story is plausible but there are no witnesses. We saw someone at the scene of the crime, seemed to be attacking or robbing the body as she lay on the ground. Unfortunately he doesn't fit the description Captain Morris has given us so we may be looking for more than one felon. Well, I must get on. I've a killer to find.'

David, his head throbbing, walked home. He passed a café and people were breakfasting outside, enjoying the June morning. He wondered at the normal sights and sounds, all happening as if there'd been no tragedy last night. The harsh reality was that there were very few people who knew or cared. He stopped abruptly and a gentleman bumped into him. They both apologised but David had suddenly realised how selfish he was being. Annabelle had an aunt and uncle and she may have had other relatives that loved her. He needed to go and pay his respects; explain what happened. Annabelle's servants would be able to help him find them. He turned and moved towards her house.

When he arrived the curtains were drawn but he knew someone would answer the bell. Agatha, her personal maid, opened the door. Her eyes were red with weeping and she peered at the visitor not knowing what to say. David spoke quickly to save her explanations.

'Agatha, I know about Annabelle. I loved her you know.' His eyes pricked as he saw her tears flow down her cheeks.

'Would you like to come in sir?'

'Thank you.'

She showed him into the elegant lounge and offered to get him some refreshment but he refused and came straight to the point.

'Agatha, I was with Annabelle last night at the ball, with her aunt and uncle. They went home early and I said I would walk her home but then we were attacked.' Her hand flew to her mouth but she said nothing. 'I must go and see her aunt and explain what happened. They entrusted her to me and I failed to protect her. Can you let me have their address?'

'Yes sir, I'll fetch it straight away.'

He moved restlessly around the room not seeing the family portraits, crystal chandeliers and thick velvet drapes and was almost startled when Agatha burst in holding a piece of paper out to him.

'Here you are sir. My mistress didn't have many relatives. Her husband, as you know, was killed in the war along with his two brothers, and she was an only child. I'm sure Mr and Mrs Anderson would be glad to see you sir.' He nodded, took the paper and left.

David sighed deeply, pleased to be out of the oppressive atmosphere death had brought to the household. His next visit was going to be unpleasant but it had to be done. It occurred to him he might cope better dressed in his own clothes so he went home and changed. Trying to comb his hair between the swathes of bandage he noticed deep purple bruising around his right eye and he needed a shave. Aware he was putting off the visit to the Andersons, he

46

decided to visit the barbers. Taking sufficient cash to pay for that, and a cab to go Birstwith, he went out into the street and locked his door.

It was lunchtime now, so after visiting Frederick the barber and almost enjoying the sympathy, he entered the Dog and Pheasant. He liked the barmaid there and knew she had a soft spot for him. He'd just finished his roast chicken dinner as she came up to him beaming.

'Well now, can I get you anything else? You need to keep your strength up after all you've been through.'

'Thanks, Nora, but I haven't got my usual appetite and I have a visit to make this afternoon. I ought to be going.'

'Oh. Perhaps you'll come back for dinner tonight, or just a drink. Nothing like a stiff whisky to dull the pain you know.'

'The drink sounds tempting. I might just do that,' said David standing and searching for some money. He frowned because he had only brought enough for the taxi to Birstwith, not anticipating having lunch.

'If you're a bit short at the moment I could start a tab. I know you'll be good for it. You could settle it when you come for that whisky perhaps or another day?'

'That's very kind, thank you. I'll see you tonight.' He managed a tired smile as he left.

Chapter 8

The smell of coffee wafted into the den where Jason sat with a small notebook. At the front of the book he wrote what had happened in his dreams and what he had discovered talking to Nathan Morris. Then at the back he wrote what he wanted to do next. This list included going to the library to see if there were any articles in the Harrogate local papers about the murder of an heiress in the summer, in the late 1920s. Then in the same period any article about an execution for murder of a man called '?' Morris. He was just writing a reminder to look at the register of deaths in Harrogate at that time, when the doorbell chimed.

Sonia smiled up at him and stood on her toes to kiss him. 'That's a lovely welcoming smell. I'm dying for a coffee.'

'Come and join me in the kitchen. It's really good to see you.'

Perched on a high stool Sonia looked around approvingly. 'Everything's so clean and tidy. I imagined you'd let it disintegrate, without Catherine to nag you.'

'Catherine was the tidiest one but she rarely nagged. Generally she was subtler than that. After she died I wanted to keep the house looking good for her. It would be like I was letting her down if it got dirty or really messy. Do you think that's crazy?'

'No, of course not, she'd be proud of you.'

Sonia saw his face redden and his eyes becoming moist so she hastily changed the subject. 'Tell me what's happened since I last saw you. Have you had any more dreams?'

'No just the two I told you about. Have you given them any thought?'

'Yes. The more I thought about them the more I believed they were not dreams nor were they anything to do with ghosts or spirits. I think you actually travelled back in time.'

'That's brilliant because I'm convinced the murder really happened. I told you I was spattered with blood so I had a sample tested. Do you know my friend, Phil, is a forensic scientist?' He saw her nod and continued. 'The test showed a family resemblance to a man called Nathan Morris and I visited him in Armley gaol this morning.'

'You have been busy! So what did you find out?'

'His grandfather was hanged for the murder of an heiress.'

'Really? This is very intriguing.' She paused and sipped her coffee, thinking, and for a while there was silence. 'If you've been travelling in time and you've never done it before, something must have changed. You know, ever since I arrived I've been feeling a kind of presence. I'm concentrating on it now and it's not evil. I'm sure it's benign. Have you got anything new, or rather old, in your nautical memorabilia?'

Jason stood up, suddenly excited and held out his hand to her. 'Let me show you my timer.'

He led her to his den and rushed to the shelf.

'Don't touch it Jason!'

'Too late Sonia, but you said it was benign.'

'Benign, yes but it's also very powerful. I've never felt any aura as strong as this. There are many artefacts that can be portals to the past but a sand timer must surely be the mother of them all. Can you remember if you touched this before you had a dream?'

'The first dream happened after I cleaned it and the second one after I showed it to Phil. So if the theory is correct I'll go there again in my sleep tonight. Why do I have to go to sleep before it'll work Sonia?'

'I don't know. I'm not an authority. Perhaps it's something to do with being relaxed that makes you receptive.'

'It makes me nervous knowing it's going to happen. What if I don't wake up? Could I get stuck in nineteen twenty something?'

Sonia held up her hands as if fending him off. 'I can't answer your questions but just remember it's not an evil force. It seems to have a role for you to play but not, evidently, to save the woman. You arrive too late to do that. I wonder if it's possible to change the time you arrive? Put it down now Jason but before you go to bed pick it up again. Let's see if handling it twice makes a difference. I also think you should be careful not to pollute the past with your presence.'

'What do you mean?'

'Well, leaving something behind or taking something and bringing it here.'

'Oh, I've already done that. When I tried to save the woman I wrapped her head in my pyjama top. Perhaps I could get it back tonight.'

'I think you should try. It seems that interfering with the past is wrong but I'm not sure who authorised that. It might just be science fiction stories. Sorry I can't be more helpful.' She stood up. "I need to go now because I've a lunch date with Roger, Roger Dutton. Do you know him?' He shook his head but she didn't tell him anything more. 'I'll give you a ring tomorrow to see how you got on.'

'Don't ring me, let me ring you because I'm going sailing and it'll be an early start.' They walked to the front door together and Jason waved her off admiring the purr of the Mercedes convertible.

Talking about lunch made him feel hungry but when he opened the fridge it was almost empty. Hopefully he opened the bread bin but that had just a stale crust that was only fit for the bin. He might be good at keeping the house clean but he sorely neglected to shop efficiently.

Catherine had enjoyed cooking and had taken charge early in their marriage when she realised his culinary skills were limited to heating up a pizza. Pizza. With that idea in mind he decided to go shopping.

The supermarket closest to his house was also close to the library. Jason parked behind the store and walked through and out to the street. He was too hungry to spend hours in the library but reluctant to go home for lunch and then come out again. He solved the problem by walking to an Italian restaurant. Forty-five minutes later, replete, with the flavour of pepperoni still lingering in his mouth, Jason walked up the steps to the library.

Research of this type was new to him so he waited at the help desk until the librarian was free. He said he wanted to look at back issues of local papers that existed between 1920 and 1935. She explained that they were on microfiche and asked if he knew how to use the machine. He shook his head so she gave him a lesson and found the relevant back issues for him.

He began playing with the controls, which seemed to move illogically, but eventually he began to feel competent and started by just reading headlines. In fact he was very disappointed by the quality and found that it was impossible to read the small print. The crime took place in summer because he had not felt cold in the alley and the woman was wearing a sleeveless dress, so he looked at June, July and August. It took him a long time just searching headlines and after several frustrating hours he had only discovered that Queen Victoria had said she was going to attend the Harrogate Agricultural show and the following week she'd cancelled and the Duke of York was going instead. The paper seemed interested in nothing but social chitchat and adverts. It was disappointing but he had to admit defeat. He cleared away the reels he had used and went back to the desk.

'Was that helpful?' the librarian asked.

'Not really, I found it impossible to read the small print and there was no real news there.'

'Ah I think you might do better with the Harrogate Advertiser. You've been looking at the Harrogate Herald and that generally covered society functions. If you decide to come again ring first and book some time then you can be sure of a machine. You were very lucky today there was a vacancy.' Jason said he would, thanked her and walked to the supermarket. He found it difficult to concentrate on what to buy and wandered up and down the aisles listlessly.

'You've not made much progress,' said a familiar voice. It was Phil pushing a trolley laden with goods. Jason looked at his own meagre effort and grinned.

'Hi Phil. I had a pizza for lunch, not hungry so no incentive to fill up on goodies.'

'Well you probably don't need much, assuming we eat in the pub again tomorrow. Are you still up for a sail? I fancy giving those youngsters a bit of competition and it forecasts quite a blow.'

'Yes, no problem and it's my turn to drive. Shall I pick you up around nine?'

They chatted for a few moments and when Phil walked off to the checkout Jason felt a surge of energy caused by this encounter and the prospect of racing tomorrow. He quickly filled his trolley with bread, butter, cheese and ham and even bought fruit and salad with a view to eating healthily. Heavy people carry a big disadvantage when racing. He grinned as he imagined Catherine, eyebrows raised, at his choice.

Back home he unpacked his food, made a mug of tea and took it into his den. He wondered how Sonia could feel the presence of the timer, even in the kitchen. He felt nothing unusual and yet he was the one travelling in time. Phil had handled the timer and he never mentioned strange dreams. Perhaps only the owner was privileged, or cursed, to venture into the past. He opened his notebook and wrote about the research in the library and Sonia's idea to handle the timer twice. As he wrote anxiety waved over him. Would he be able to sleep at all knowing what would happen when he did?

Later he made himself a sandwich and watched television, but the anxiety stayed with him. Just before going to bed he went back into the den and picked up the timer. He almost expected it to vibrate or glow but it was as inert as every other time he'd handled it.

In the bedroom, laying down fully clothed, he shut his eyes but, as predicted, it was not easy to relax and he resorted to a sleeping pill.

He was in the alley. There was no running figure, or scream but he could hear voices. He moved towards the light but hovered in the shadows as he saw a couple facing each other. They were talking earnestly and the man had one arm resting on her waist and held a silver topped cane in the other. They were both in evening dress and Jason recognised the clothes of the woman he'd been unable to save.

Suddenly a figure ran towards them with a raised club. Jason was paralysed as he watched the assault take place and everything playing out as it did before but, just as he was about to move towards the woman to see if he could help her, another man walked past him and he saw, with a shock, that it was himself. He watched the figure take off his nightshirt and attempt to revive the woman. The policeman arrived and his own figure disappeared.

Jason shrank back into the shadows as the doctor knelt beside her and then he heard footsteps coming from behind him. The man in evening dress returned and stood very close to him, also watching and quietly crying. The poor man was obviously shocked and could see nothing but the macabre business being played out before him as the hearse arrived and his beautiful companion was placed inside it.

52

The policeman lingered after the body had gone and picked up something from the pavement. With a shrinking feeling of dread Jason realised it was his pyjama T-shirt. He would never be able to retrieve it now. He'd committed the, apparently unforgivable, sin of interfering with the past.

The scene cleared of people and the gentleman standing close to him moved slowly back down the alley.

It was all over but Jason was still there. The timer had failed to return him to the present. What should he do now?

Chapter 9

Finding a hansom cab was not difficult and soon David was driving up through the imposing gates of the manor. He had never been there before and was impressed. The lawn was neat, flowerbeds were a mass of colour and the garden was flanked with mature trees. The manor itself was Yorkshire stone, double fronted but not huge. David felt a twinge of envy as he surveyed it all, then turned back to the driver and asked to be collected in an hour. The cab drove away and David watched it, reluctant to see the elderly couple he had met for the first time the night before. He turned with a sigh and pulled the bell on the front door.

A maid opened it and said, 'The master saw you arrive, sir, and asked me to show you into the study.' He followed her and found the study empty of people. It was small and cosy with two winged easy chairs on either side of the fireplace. There were laden bookshelves and watercolours on almost every spare inch of the wall. One picture caught his eye and as he moved closer to study it he realised with a shock that it was Annabelle. She was wearing a summer dress and her smiling face was framed by a straw hat. She was holding a basket of flowers and the trees and lawn behind her suggested it was painted in the garden of the manor.

David turned as he heard the door open and Mr Anderson entered alone. This would make it easier and he hoped the interview would be short. He stepped forward, hand out-stretched, but there was no move to take it so he dropped it to his side. 'I had to come to say how deeply sorry I am to have been unable to protect Annabelle. You entrusted her to me and I couldn't save her.'

There was a half sob, half choking noise but Mr Harrison said nothing.

David stumbled on, 'I loved her you know. I had just asked her to marry me when we were attacked by a robber with a club.' He touched his injury as if to support his statement. 'I've been to the police and given a description of the man.' His voice dwindled to a whisper. 'I'm so desperately sorry.'

Mr Harrison managed to speak at last. 'It must have been difficult for you to come here. My wife and I are in deep shock. Annabelle meant everything to us, just like a daughter. It may be that you did all you could but in our hearts we can't forgive you, or ourselves. I would like you to go now and would prefer it if you didn't come again or attend the funeral.'

He left the room and David, stunned, stood motionless. The maid arrived and without another word he followed her to the door. It was too soon for the cab so he walked to the main gates and stood there waiting. It had been far worse than he had expected.

When he eventually arrived home from his visit to the Andersons he felt depressed and his mood was not improved when he saw he had a visitor. It was Detective Peterson. David invited him inside and offered him a seat.

'No I'll stand thank you this won't take long. I'll get straight to the point. At the scene of the crime a garment was found. Could you identify what it is and tell me if it belongs to you?' He unwrapped a brown paper parcel to reveal a kind of short-sleeved vest stained deeply with blood.

'I've never seen it before. I don't know where it came from or how it can be anything to do with Annabelle or me.'

'Well you see we found it wrapped around her head as if someone had crudely tried to bandage it. That person wasn't you then?'

'No I told you I ran after the attacker. I wasn't thinking straight. I know I should have stayed with Annabelle. But...' He paused and Peterson looked at him sharply. 'Have you thought of something?'

'I came back to her to see if she had woken up and there was a man kind of astride her pushing on her chest. I think he was trying to help her. Before I could challenge him the policeman blew his whistle and the man, this sounds ridiculous, he disappeared.'

'Can you describe him?'

'He was naked on the top and wore some shorts. He had bare feet. His hair was dark and he was slim and young, perhaps thirty.'

'That's excellent. I thought there might be another felon. Thank you Captain. I assume this garment was his.'

After a few minutes he was ready to go and David showed him to the door. He turned as he stepped onto the pavement. 'You've been really helpful but I may need to speak to you again so please don't go out of town.'

David shut the door and leant on it. This was too much. He wanted to hit something or scream. In the end he cried, all his grief pouring out until he was exhausted. When he felt capable of moving he washed his face, shocked by the haggard appearance he saw in the mirror. The need for comfort and sympathy prompted him to take enough cash from his drawer to pay off his tab and walk to the pub.

The Dog and Pheasant was busy serving food and beer. The atmosphere was warm and welcoming. In fact it was a little too warm and many people had spilled out into the street and were chatting and drinking outside. David squeezed his way to the bar and ordered a beer from a smiling Nora. 'You're back then. Phew it's warm. I'm off shortly, having done the lunchtime stint I only work till nine. You've just time to get a bite to eat then you and me could go somewhere quiet and cool.' She laughed loudly as if she had made a huge joke and David smiled back. It was impossible not to like her sense of fun and her voluptuous body. He realised he was staring at her large breasts almost thrusting out of her low cut dress, desiring her. His emotions threatened to overwhelm him again. Nora promised to bring his pork pie over to him, nodding towards a small table that had just become vacant. He sat down feeling confused and depressed.

A few moments later she arrived with his food. Her breast rubbed against his shoulder as she placed the plate in front of him. 'I thought you'd like a chunk of crusty bread and some pickles to soak up that whisky I promised you. Can't have you so drunk you fall asleep on me!' She laughed loudly again and left him to eat.

The food, beer and whisky blunted the edge of his grief and he began to look forward to nine o'clock.

They walked out into the cooler evening air towards Nora's rooms. She had the top floor of a town house not far from the pub.

56

They arrived, puffing with the exertion of climbing two flights of stairs, and Nora unlocked her door. The air smelt stale and dishes were piled in and around the sink in the kitchen.

'I'll have to speak to me maid, she's not pulling her weight.' She laughed again and then gave a little squeak as David put his arms around her and roughly handled her breasts. She pushed his hands away and turned towards him. 'Don't be so hasty. We'll get there. I just need to freshen up after all that heat. Sit down a minute until I'm ready.'

He did as he was told and then stood again and wandered around the small room hoping she'd be quick. When Nora appeared again she was wearing nothing but a silky nightdress and she expertly helped David remove his clothes. There was little finesse about their coupling and it was all over too quickly. Nora felt cheated and said he should stay the night so they could have another go in the morning. David wanted to leave. He had had his need fulfilled and he felt guilty. 'I can't stop the night Nora. I promised the police to be at home so they could talk to me again.'

'The police, are you in trouble then?'

'No. It's in case I can think of anything else to help find Annabelle's killer.'

'Oh. Well perhaps we can do this another night.'

David sighed. 'I'm sorry Nora. I should never have come. I shouldn't…'

'No you shouldn't!' Nora was shouting now. 'You've used me, had your bit of fun and now you want to go. I'm not good enough for you. Well you're not just going. You owe me.'

'You're right, but I don't have any cash.'

'I'm not a whore but I would've accepted cash, seeing as how you've treated me so bad. What have you got?' David pulled out his pocket watch and held it out to her. She took it and held it close to the light. 'That's a good solid silver watch - must be worth a bit. It'll do but don't come into the Dog and Pheasant again.'

David slunk out of the flat, stumbled down the staircase in the dark, quietly went out of the front door and filled his lungs with the fresh night air. He walked home regretting the loss of his watch and the whole sordid, brief affair.

When he'd gone Nora grinned with delight and looked closer at the watch. It was a beauty and she decided to hide it in her special box secreted under a floorboard. Kicking aside the thin mat she knelt, put her fingers in the large knothole, and pulled. It was not unusual for customers in the pub or in her room to pay with trinkets and she had become something of a collector. She fingered the silver bracelet, pearl earrings and now she added the pocket watch. Her knees began to ache so she put everything back and stood with a grunt.

The box was for a rainy day because she risked pregnancy whenever urges like the one that night came upon her. If she got pregnant she would lose her job and she had no relatives to help her. The thought of having a child was pleasing but it was unlikely anyone would marry her, being well past her prime. She sighed, looking at the mess around her, decided she would clean up tomorrow and went back to bed.

David walked home in a mood close to despair. He sunk onto his bed fully clothed but sleep was impossible. His stupid actions in the last few days flooded through his mind and he felt the need to do something but there was nothing he could do. Eventually he got up, washed and changed into clean clothes. Feeling a little more civilised he decided to go out for an early breakfast but there was an ominous loud knock on the door. He opened it and faced the detective again.

'Good morning sir, I would like you to accompany me, and my constable here, to the station. We have some questions we need to ask you.'

'More questions; I really can't tell you anything else.'

'We'd prefer you came quietly, sir, or you'll force me to arrest you.'

'I'll fetch my hat.' David followed the two men as they walked briskly to the police station, wondering if things could ever be worse than they were now.

Chapter 10

2016

Sonia wriggled, turned over and plumped the pillows again but although she flopped back and shut her eyes, sleep eluded her. Finally, exasperated, she sat up and put the bedside light on. Relaxing was impossible knowing what Jason was intending to do and not knowing if he was safe. She felt guilty she had encouraged him to return to collect his pyjama top and frightened that touching the timer twice might produce an extended stay, or worse. There were so many possibilities of disaster rushing through her mind she could bear it no longer and got out of bed.

Sonia dressed in a comfortable, designer tracksuit and left her house quietly. It felt strange to be going out in the dark when everyone else was sleeping. The air felt fresh and she walked briskly, enjoying the activity and the sense of purpose. The walk took her about thirty minutes and as she approached Jason's home she slowed with uncertainty.

If he was safely asleep he would be annoyed at being woken. He had said she should wait for a phone call. She stood, irresolute, for a while and then decided to ring the bell and risk an angry reception. There was no response so she tried again. The bell echoed through the house and he must have heard it so she went around the back.

Years ago Catherine had brought her into the house that way when she had lost her keys. It was possible the spare was still under the plant pot. She felt about and was rewarded as her hand grabbed the back door key. The kitchen door opened easily and after some fumbling she found the light.

'Jason.' She paused, listening and then called again. Sonia moved into the hall, making no attempt to be quiet now and ran up the stairs. She stopped at the bedroom door, feeling like an intruder, but pushed it open and moved towards the bed. There was a mound as if it had an occupant but that occupant had been spirited away.

Fearful that all her worst thoughts were coming true she went down to the study. She was about to put the light on but saw the 'nautical nonsense' cabinet was glowing. The light was emanating from the sand timer. Bending down she peered closely without touching it and saw some writing and some symbols that she was sure had not been visible before. Helping herself to paper and a pen from the desk she copied what she could see. Then she took the paper to the desk, sat down and put on the reading light.

VI SERVO
APDEMR
OINCIU
TLIEOM

Well the first bit's easy, she thought. It's the symbol for female followed by the Roman numeral for six. Servo is to serve, so the timer helps women, but I've no idea what the other letters mean. Turning the letters around on the second line she could form the word 'dream' but there was a P left. The bottom line also held the word time but again there were superfluous letters.

Sonia was tired, anxious and completely stumped. Roger could figure this out, she thought, so she switched on Jason's computer and emailed him. He was a mathematical genius and dear friend who loved puzzles. He might solve it quickly because he often rose early.

Moving into the kitchen Sonia made an instant coffee and some toast. She brought them back to the study and curled up in Jason's armchair listening for sounds of his return or an email. The email alert woke her, she jerked and spilt some cold coffee. How could she have gone to sleep holding a cup? How could she have nodded off with Jason stuck in the past? She hauled herself stiffly out of the chair and went to the computer. Roger had written back.

'What are you doing up so early Sonia? Anyway I found your problem interesting but not satisfying. The number six could refer to the sixth month, June, named after the Roman goddess Juno, daughter of Saturn. She was also wife and sister of Jupiter, mother of

Mars and goddess of women. That naturally tallies with the symbol. The other words are an anagram of the Latin words, 'admonitio' and 'periculem'. The former means warning and the latter danger. The inscription seems to suggest a talisman for the protection of women. Where did you find it? Was it on an amulet or, even more exciting, a sword?'

Sonia had no intention of explaining the source of the inscription. Roger was lovely but only believed what could be proved scientifically. He would never sanction the idea of time travel. She thought for a moment and then wrote,

I knew you would solve it, thank you. I'm really looking forward to our dinner date.
Sonia x

Sonia hoped that changing the subject to their next date would stop him pondering the source of the inscription. Roger was becoming more than just a casual friend and she knew he would now be thinking of her.

She turned the computer off and decided to check that Jason had not returned while she was asleep. The bed was still empty so she returned to the study and sat back in his armchair with a pen and paper. It would help her organise her thoughts if she wrote down the possibilities.

1. I could touch the timer in the hope that it would break the connection and bring Jason back to the present.

2. If that misfired it might whisk me back into the past.

3. The timer was dedicated to women so whatever happened I would be safe.

4. All the above are useless because I don't have the confidence to try.

There was nothing to be done except wait, hope or even pray for his safe return. Her eyes drooped and she surrendered again to sleep.

Catherine was saying, 'It's a new thing called the Well Woman Clinic, just a health check. Anyway I'll only be half an hour or so.'

The front door slammed and Sonia jumped up and ran to the lounge window. She could clearly see Catherine's head twisted to look behind as she backed the car out of the drive.

This must be a dream, Sonia thought, and made her way back to the study. On the desk was a digital clock and calendar that showed it was 10am on December 23rd.

The shock woke her up and she found herself in Jason's armchair. Her heart was pumping with anxiety. The dream had been so real. She looked at the clock again, 5.45am, June 21st.

She had been asleep for several hours so was Jason back now? She ran up to his bedroom but he was still in the past. She looked out of the bedroom window as if she was waiting for him to appear, walking down the street, or drawing up in a car. It was clearly dawn but dull, raining gently. Sonia returned to the study and looked at the timer. It was comforting that it was still glowing because it seemed he could return as long as it glowed. That was pure supposition but it helped her to believe it. Sitting back in the armchair convinced that sleep was impossible, her eyes began to close and this time it was a dreamless sleep.

Jason stood, uncertain what to do but then decided if the timer had not returned him to the present he must still have a task to complete. That must be because he had contaminated the past so the T-shirt must be retrieved. The police had collected it so he would go to the station and offer himself as an eyewitness.

He knew where the police station was in his own time but had it been there in 1929? The song, 'If you want to know the time ask a policeman,' kept churning through his mind as he walked. Suddenly, ahead of him, he saw two policemen walking slowly side by side so he followed their beat, assuming they would eventually return to the station. He was lucky because they turned a couple of corners and were there. It was not in the same place as the current one but that was now irrelevant. He waited a few minutes, took a deep breath and went in.

'Can I help you sir?' The sergeant behind the desk raised an eyebrow to encourage a response and then Jason found his voice.

'I saw a thug, armed with a club attacking a couple this evening, in Oxford Street. So I'm a witness.'

The sergeant drew a form towards him. 'Well, well that is very interesting. Can I take down some particulars? Name?'

'Jason, Jason Brownlow.'

'Unusual name, parents interested in the classics were they? Address?'

Jason gave his real address, hoping his house existed in 1929. It seemed to pass muster as the sergeant lifted a flap in the counter and invited Jason to follow him. He was offered a chair in a room containing just two on either side of a small table.

'I'll fetch Detective Peterson. He'll be very interested to hear what you have to say.'

Jason felt anxious. He was uncomfortable on the hard wooden chair and wanted to stand and walk about. Before he could put this desire into practice the detective arrived. Jason looked at the slight figure smiling at him, with bright intelligent eyes, and knew he needed to be careful of this man.

'Thanks, Sergeant, you can leave this to me and return to your post.' The sergeant nodded and left, closing the door behind him. Jason fought a strong desire to escape but held himself in check.

'So, Mr Brownlow, you saw Mrs Larkin attacked and killed this evening. Perhaps you'd tell me about it.'

'I don't know Mrs Larkin but I saw a lady and gentleman talking in Oxford Street and then a man crept up on them wielding a club. He raised it to hit the man but the lady screamed and as the gentleman turned the blow partly hit him but then hit the lady on the front of her head.'

'What happened next?'

'The armed man, seeing he'd only stunned the gentleman, robbed him and ran down the street. After a moment, when he couldn't rouse the woman, the gentleman ran after him. I tried to help the lady but I couldn't revive her. Then I heard the police whistle, panicked and ran. Later I realised I ought to come in and see you.'

'Hmm. Can you describe the man with the club?'

'The light was poor and it all happened very quickly. He was not wearing a hat and his hair was dark. He was a similar height and build to me. He was wearing a collarless shirt, no coat.'

'When you tried to help Mrs Larkin what did you do? I took off my top and tried to stop the bleeding with it.'

'Well, that is interesting. Thank you for the information.'

Jason began to stand, assuming the interview was over, but Detective Peterson put up a hand and gently pressed him back onto his seat.

'I can't let you go, Mr Brownlow, until I've made a few more enquiries. You see I'm thinking you may be an exceptionally clever man, who has accidently murdered a woman and who hopes to place suspicion elsewhere. We will detain you in a cell until we have more information. You say you removed your top but you are fully clothed, albeit strangely. No, I must keep you here.'

He stood, opened the door and shouted for the sergeant who came running.

'Show Mr Brownlow to a cell please and get him a cup of tea.'

Jason was led down the corridor and a cell was unlocked for him to enter.

'Make yourself at home. The tea won't be long.'

The door clanged and the key rattled in the lock. Jason sat on the bed, hoping it was flea free, and looked bleakly at the bare walls. What was he going to do? He had not got his T-shirt, he was a prime suspect in the murder and he was still in the past. The key turned in the lock. Jason hoped it was his tea and not another interview but then he woke up in his bed, in the present.

Jason wanted to cry with relief and vowed he would never touch the timer again. It was light, nearly six o'clock so he got up and went down to the kitchen to put the kettle on. There was bread, butter and marmalade out on the worktop. Someone was in the house and had helped him or her self to breakfast. He went slowly into the lounge but, finding it empty, he approached the study. When he opened the door and saw Sonia asleep in his chair he tiptoed out and took another cup out of the cupboard.

Something told him she might prefer coffee after such an uncomfortable night so he put the filter pot on. The bread looked inviting so he made a plateful of toast then poured the coffee and took the laden tray into the study. As he placed the tray down on the desk Sonia woke, gave a cry and leapt up. She threw her arms around him and sobbed. 'I thought you were stuck in the past for ever. I've been so scared. I can't tell you how glad I am to see you.'

'I must admit I was getting scared too but everything's fine now and I have a lot to tell you, so let's have breakfast and talk.'

Jason went first and his adventures were punctuated by little gasps from Sonia as she realised what danger he'd been in. Then she related the glowing of the timer, the coded inscription and finally her own dream.

'The thing is Jason. I didn't touch the timer so I can't be sure it wasn't a dream.'

'I'm certain you went back into the past and I think touching it was not necessary because it was already awake and working. I have relived that moment Catherine left the house, so unaware that she would never return and you have just quoted the exact words that were said. You could not have known that.'

'Oh, that's really creepy. The timer's so powerful. I think you're playing with fire. Remember, if it's designed to protect women it may not care what happens to a man.' She stood, stretched, and yawned. 'This has been one hell of a night Jason. I'm not sure if I'm going home to bed or if I'm going to have a shower and start the day. Either way I'm leaving now and please tell me if you decide to use the timer again.'

She went to the door and turned to hug him before she left. Jason shut it behind her, changed into his jogging gear and went for a run. It was Sunday and he'd arranged to go sailing so he would not be too long. He pounded the pavement, deep in thought. He had vowed not to go back in time again but his shirt was still there. Did that matter? If he went back he could, probably would, be arrested but if the timer wanted him to help a woman he had not achieved that. He stopped musing and worked his way back home. He needed a quick shower before he met Phil. It was quite windy, force 4 to 5 in his estimate. They should have an excellent race or two.

Chapter 11

The interview room was stark and footsteps echoed. A constable stood by the door and David felt like a trapped animal.

'I loved Annabelle. I don't understand why you think I would kill her. What would I gain?

The inspector was silent. Perhaps he hoped by letting the prisoner talk a confession or a slip would be made.

'What more can I say?' The silence was tangible. 'I walked her home and we stopped and that's when I asked her to marry me.'

Finally the inspector spoke. 'What did she say?'

'She said she was scared to marry because the death of Mr Larkin had been so painful she couldn't face being hurt like that again.'

'So you were spurned. How did you feel? Angry? Did you want to hit her? You had a cane.'

David vehemently shook his head, protesting his innocence. 'I was just going to gather her up in my arms to reassure her of my love when she screamed and we were both hit.' He put his hand up to his ear.

The interview continued and then the exhausted prisoner was escorted to a cell. David sat on the hard bed, shoulders hunched, holding his head in his hands. Tears flowed as he felt sorry for failing to protect Annabelle and sorry for himself. He brushed them away. His brain went over the events of the attack and the interview. He couldn't understand why they suspected him. Surely they didn't think he hit himself on the head after hitting Annabelle? It was all a misunderstanding. They had sent a message to his solicitor, Robert Finch. He was a good man. Robert would make them see sense.

Eventually David fell asleep and was woken by the sound of the key turning in the lock. The cell door swung open with a clang and a constable came in with an enamel mug of tea and some toast.

'Morning Captain, the inspector says to eat this quick because Mr Finch is due here in ten minutes. So look lively.'

The smell of the toast was enticing and it seemed a long time since he had eaten anything so he consumed all of it. Then he washed his face in the grimy bowl. He had just finished when a man entered the cell but it was not Robert. The man introduced himself as the duty doctor and proceeded to clean his wound. It was no longer bleeding so he did not put another dressing on it.

Robert was shocked when he saw the swollen face, the wound and bluish bruising. They talked alone for some time and Robert, far from being reassuring, said he really needed a witness because his story was weak. He asked him if he was sure they were alone when they stopped because the police seemed to have a man in custody that said he saw it all. This was good news. If his story were corroborated he would be free. David said again he had seen no one, until he returned from trying to catch the thief but the street was badly lit so he may have been mistaken.

Suddenly there was shouting, the sound of running feet and a cell door clanging. Robert left him to find out what was going on. He returned looking serious.

'It seems the witness has disappeared. He was apparently locked in a cell last night but has gone this morning. There's mayhem out there because the sergeant is certain he turned the key in the lock but the man has gone. This doesn't bode well for you David. It's also very strange because he came forward of his own volition. So why did he run away?'

David was removed to a secure prison in Leeds awaiting trial. Weeks went by and Robert Finch's visits became less frequent. He had put advertisements in the Harrogate papers asking for the mysterious witness to come forward but there had been no response. The police had taken statements from Caruthers and had done some scientific work on the bloodstains on David's bandage and clothes.

Caruthers' valet had made a good job of cleaning the evening suit so it had yielded little but his shoes still had blood on them. Robert was not sure if it was possible to find out much from blood other than the broad groups A B and O, but it was worrying and it was not looking good for his client.

David couldn't believe they would find him guilty but, as every day passed, with nothing to add to his defence, he sunk into despair. He ate little and his body shrank away from his clothes.

In November, nearly five months after the attack, Caruthers came to see him. The warden stepped back after unlocking the door and his friend came in, hand extended and then dropped it in shock. 'My God... You look so thin I can hardly recognize you.'

'It's good to see you Caruthers. You look just the same.' He attempted a smile but it looked like a rictus in a skull.

'The police have interviewed me several times. I told them what a great chap you were and how much you adored Annabelle. I'm to appear as a witness in your trial but I don't know if I'll be much help.

'Just tell the truth about that night. That's all you can do. You have been a good friend and I want to thank you for supporting me, in case I don't get the chance to see you again.'

'What do you mean? You mustn't give up. You've got an excellent council and I'm sure the jury will find you not guilty. Now is there anything you need that I can get sent in? Perhaps a book to read?'

David shook his head. 'There's nothing to do in here but I can't seem to concentrate on anything. The only thing I need and crave, is to be able to leave here a free man.'

Caruthers nodded sympathetically. They talked a little more but the conversation was stilted and awkward. Eventually Caruthers sighed and stood. 'Well if there's nothing I can do I'll go. Please eat more even if the food's poor. You'll need all your strength to cope with the trial.' He extended his hand; David shook it and watched him go through the door out into the world.

Would he ever feel the fresh air again, he thought and did he care?

The weeks passed and the trial was imminent. David felt numb and fatalistic. Then he had an unexpected visitor, Nora from The Dog and Pheasant. She had made no effort with her appearance looking very round and solid with a stained blouse straining at the buttons over her huge breasts.

'Prison doesn't agree with you does it David,' was her greeting.

'You get used to it Nora. You seem to be blooming.'

'Well I thought I'd come and see you, in case they find you guilty, to tell you I'm pregnant.'

'Oh. I thought you were just… So why did you want to tell me?'

'Oh don't be so naïve! I'm five months gone so that makes it your brat. Yours! I'm not a tart. So what are you going to do about supporting us? Thanks to you I've lost me job. How am I going to work with a baby?'

David looked at her and shrugged. 'I don't know what to say. I can't help you Nora. I don't have any money.'

'Don't give me that, Captain. You're a gentleman. You have private means and I want some of it.' She paused for breath and David began to recover from the initial shock.

'Nora, listen, all my assets have been taken and used to fund my court case. I have to pay my solicitor and the KC. They've taken all my possessions and my army pension. I am as poor as you and if I ever get out of prison I'll be homeless and penniless. I cannot help you.'

She stood up angrily. 'So that's it then, nothing. Well I hope they hang you!' She shouted this and the words lingered in the air as she was let out of the cell.

David had stood when she did but now felt weak and quickly sat down. He was to be a father and he couldn't help his child. He may not even see it if the verdict went against him. He wondered how quickly a death sentence was carried out after the trial. Was it usually the following day? He hoped so. There would be no point in prolonging his suffering. He was ready now.

On the morning of the trial David was given clean clothes and a larger breakfast than usual.

'So, George, is this the condemned man's extra privileges?'

'No, Captain, don't talk like that. We always give prisoners a bit extra on court days because it's hard, very hard. You're nowt but skin and bone and you need to keep your strength up.'

'Well thank you I appreciate your concern and I'll do my best to eat it but I've little appetite.'

It was not long before he was led out of the prison and taken to Leeds Crown Court. He briefly felt the cold air before being ushered into the van. The journey was short and entering the court was shocking. There was so much noise and several people booed and hissed as he was led to his seat. Robert Finch was sitting near him with Philip Keene, his KC. They both acknowledged him with a nod and looked very serious. He looked around and saw Annabelle's uncle in the gallery and one or two acquaintances. He felt nervous now and wished the trial would get underway. Robert had said Justice Sylvester was fair and he was lucky to be brought before him. At that moment a voice boomed, 'All rise,' and everybody stood as the judge came in.

Chapter 12

2016

Sonia began to walk home, her brain teeming with muddled thoughts. Why did it seem acceptable for Jason to sleep himself into the past but not her? The dream of Catherine had seemed real and Jason believed it was. Why did she find that so hard to accept? It was probably something to do with being out of control, an unusual state for her to be in. If she did accept it as true then perhaps the timer was showing her a task and that task could only be saving Catherine from having the accident.

The consequences of such an act needed serious consideration. She knew nothing about Annabelle Larkin and Captain David Morris. To her they were just like characters in a novel, but she knew Catherine, Jason and some of their friends and family. If they changed the past then everything that had happened since Catherine's death would not have happened. How far did this reach? Would it turn back time for the whole world, just England or just for those people that knew her? The answers were unknown. If Jason went back eight months he would not have attempted to save Annabelle. It would also mean she might not have met her Roger. She thought about Roger and smiled as she remembered how they met.

Just after the funeral Sonia had gone on a cruise, booked months ago, to South America. It began in Rio and went to the 'bottom of the world', Cape Horn and finished in Santiago. Roger was also travelling alone and had been on her dining table the first night. Within moments they were chatting like old friends. He walked her back to her cabin after the show and they talked about the trips they had booked. The following day the ship docked at Montevideo in Uruguay and they agreed to meet for breakfast and then explore the city together.

It was very hot and they had walked several miles when Roger suggested they stopped for a drink. He had changed some money on the ship and treated her to a cold white wine spritzer. She sipped her drink, enjoying the moment, sitting under an umbrella on the pavement.

'Isn't this just heaven?' she said. 'It's hard to believe while we're sweltering in this heat in England everyone's shivering.'

'Delightful isn't it? I'm looking forward to showing off my tan to my friends back home.'

'Where's home?'

'Northallerton, North Yorkshire, not all that far from York.'

'I know exactly where that is because I live in Harrogate. We're practically neighbours. What a coincidence.' Sonia smiled at him and they walked back to the ship arm in arm. Knowing they lived close to each other enabled them to take each day as it came, with no sense of urgency and their friendship blossomed.

One morning they left the ship on a tender to do an off-road driving trip on the Falkland Islands having anchored just off Port Stanley.

'Have you been off-roading before?' she asked.

Roger grinned, 'Just a bit. I used to own an old Range Rover and joined a club. It was great fun and sometimes challenging with very steep ascents and descents.' He was describing this with his hands as he spoke. 'But the best times were when the ground was slippery with mud or it was really deep snow.'

'Oh, well you're going with a complete novice so I hope I won't embarrass you by squealing.'

The trip was just for an afternoon and they had time to wander around the colourful town. They asked another tourist to take their photograph, posing together inside the famous whalebone arch, by the church.

The tour began in a minibus along a road. They stopped and moved into Land Rovers that turned off the road and slowly lumbered and bounced over the tussocks and hollows. They were heading for the sea and Sonia enjoyed it, feeling no need to squeal.

Their destination was to see a colony of penguins. There were hundreds of them, standing close together on the grass, the warm breeze ruffling their feathers. Sonia loved the fluffy baby ones and

Roger spotted several different species. They were told to stay as long as they liked but once they had finished taking photographs they could walk over a hill to a hut where afternoon tea would be available.

'Isn't this amazing?' said Roger. 'We are so far from home, standing in the sunshine on a beach filled with penguins in a little piece of Britain. Are you ready to sample English tea?'

Sonia smiled, 'I can't wait.'

They walked together, holding hands but at the brow of the hill Sonia dropped his hand and put hers to her cheeks. 'Just look at that.' The side of the hut had a huge old orange penguin book on it. 'It's wonderful! Come on I can almost smell the tea.'

It was a true delight. The tea was organised by the local WI and they had delicate china cups and homemade cakes. After her third cup of tea and second scone with red crowberry jam Sonia sighed with pleasure. 'This has been so lovely, Roger. I don't think I'd have dared to do this trip if you hadn't persuaded me and look what I'd have missed.' She waved her hand to encompass the blue sky, the rippling waves, sea birds soaring and the WI tea hut.

'I've enjoyed it too,' he said, 'But what's made it even better for me is doing it with you. You've never driven off-road before but you just rolled with it like a pro and I felt proud of you. That tall American woman grumbled all the way.' They both giggled and began to walk back to their Land Rover.

When they were back on board the ship they separated, having agreed to meet for drinks before dinner. Sonia had cruised before on her own but the experience was greatly enhanced now she had met Roger.

Lying on her bed, a book beside her, she shut her eyes to sleep but found she was reliving the day and knew she really wanted to keep seeing him when the holiday ended. She hoped he felt the same.

On their last night aboard ship Sonia dared to pose the question. ' Roger, we get off tomorrow, back to chilly England. I need to ask you something.' She looked into his eyes and was encouraged by his smile. 'Would you like to meet me for a drink or something?'

His smile became even broader. 'I was going to ask you the same thing but afraid to, in case you weren't keen. It shows you're braver than me!' They laughed, exchanged details and made a date on the first Sunday after their return, to have lunch at a pub they both knew.

That first date was a great success. It felt like the beginning of a real friendship, not just a holiday romance. Regular Sunday lunches happened after that, trips to the theatre in Leeds and sometimes a healthy walk on the moors.

Sonia adored his quirky sense of humour and thought him a real gentleman. If she had any reservations about his personality she felt he lacked imagination. She wondered what he would say if she told him about the sand timer. It was an idle thought because, lovely though he was, this was way out of his realm of understanding.

Thinking of Roger made her look at her watch and hurry. She needed to shower and change into something smart, perhaps the green swirly skirt and the plain matching jacket. Roger liked her to look feminine, not keen on trousers, 'You have shapely legs so why not show them,' he'd said. It was a compliment but made him seem a little old-fashioned.

Sonia emerged an hour later looking fresh and pretty, no hint of her disturbed night showing on her carefully made-up face. She was determined to enjoy herself and shelve all thoughts of time travel and Jason. He was probably going sailing and nothing else would happen until night. Better not to think about that.

Roger arrived at the pub just before her and stood against his car enjoying the sunshine. He waved as she got out and moved towards her. She watched him in the wing mirror and felt a flutter of excitement, more usual in a teenager. He was taller than her, trim with a slightly greying beard. He reminded her of Sean Connery, without the Scottish twang and Roger had no trouble pronouncing an s either. Then he was with her. They kissed and moved into the pub arm in arm.

They began with a soft drink and read the menu. Sonia chose the chicken and Roger the beef. While they waited for the food to come Roger said, 'That was an interesting puzzle you sent me and I'm really intrigued. Why didn't you tell me where you found it? '

'Oh, it's not very exciting. I've mentioned Jason to you, the one whose wife died.' Roger nodded. 'Well he's a keen sailor and collects things to do with old ships like compasses, telescopes, you know. He's got a sand timer and the inscription was on that, odd really.'

'Yes but not that peculiar because in the olden days sailors had all kinds of weird superstitions. They had female figureheads but thought a woman aboard could cause ill luck. I'd have liked your story better had it been a sword. Oh I think this is our lunches arriving.'

Sonia was glad to have told Roger, without revealing the power of the timer and she relaxed and enjoyed the succulent chicken.

Jason's day was not going as well as Sonia's. They had got to the lake in good time and the boat was soon rigged and ready to go. Jason won the toss for who was to helm but it was not a good choice. They moved towards the start and he went about too late, crossing the line after several others.

'What are you doing?' shouted Phil, 'That was rubbish timing. We'll never make that up.' He was right. They managed to pass several boats during the course of the race but ended in third place.

'Sorry, I didn't sleep well. I'll do better in the next one.' They came second and Phil began to smile again. After lunch they entered the third race but Jason was having difficulty concentrating and after achieving fifth place they decided to call it a day. They de-rigged the boat and hauled it up the ramp to its place in the boat park, hardly talking.

'I said I'm sorry Phil. I know winning means a lot to you and it used to be really important to me too but at the moment I'm no asset to you. If you want to find someone else to crew for you then feel free. I promise it will not affect our friendship.'

'I don't want anyone else,' muttered Phil, 'and, anyway, I can't think of any light youngsters who could give me a weight advantage.'

'Well if you do, don't hesitate to ask them. Let me know and if you're unsuccessful I'll crew for you next week.' There was no more to say and the atmosphere was strained as they drove home.

Jason felt wretched. He hated having fallen out with Phil and was annoyed with himself for not doing well. He decided to do some cleaning, washing and other basic chores because he never felt like doing those things after work. Much later, after a microwave ready meal he took his coffee into his study to check his emails. There was one from Phil, apologising for his irritability and one from Sonia reminding him to tell her if he decided to touch the timer that night.

He rang her. 'Sonia? Hi. Have you had a good day?'

'Lovely, thank you, despite the lack of sleep. I had lunch with Roger, followed by a walk in Valley Gardens, very Sunday afternoon-ish. What about you? Good sail?'

'Not really, I made a hash of it and Phil was cross. But I give myself Brownie points for coming home, cleaning and doing the washing.'

'Very domesticated. Did you get my email?'

'Yes, that's why I'm ringing. I've decided to handle the timer three times and risk getting arrested again. I don't want you to worry about me and come over full of anxiety. I want you to get a good night's sleep and I'll ring you before I go to work tomorrow to tell you how I got on.' There was a short silence and then Sonia sighed and promised not to panic.

He went to the timer and turned it over. As he watched the sand flow he marvelled that he could feel nothing. It just seemed an innocent, historical artefact. Returning to the computer he plugged in Catherine's memory stick. This was bound to be upsetting but he needed to see if there was anything on it he should keep. If not he was going to throw it away. All these memories of her hurt so much it was better not to keep too many reminders.

The stick held her contacts and he ran through the list just in case he had failed to inform any friend about her accident but there were no surprises. The word documents were mostly letters and there was nothing important there. The other large file was her Family Tree that she had been working on for some time. He had not been involved because she said she was going to concentrate on her side of the family first.

He opened the file and as he cast his eye over the first page a name leapt out, Annabelle Larkin, married to Maurice Larkin, died in 1929 aged 35. He worked out the relationship. She had been Catherine's Grandmother's Aunt. This was a shocking revelation. He stood, left the desk and walked to the door then walked back again. Agitation churned inside him and he felt out of control. Should he stop now?

The pacing continued as he wrestled with the decision then he walked resolutely to the timer and turned it for the second time. Moving back to the computer he 'Googled' the name Maurice Larkin and was rewarded with several entries but they all referred to an historian who wrote about wars and his dates didn't fit. He wondered if Who's Who was now on line. It was but revealed nothing and Jason was getting tired. It was time to make a hot drink to take to bed.

In the kitchen he chose hot chocolate then carried it back into the den and turned the timer once more. He carried the chocolate upstairs and decided not to undress. He even kept his trainers on, confident that he was going to go back in time again.

The sleeping pill combined with hot chocolate, relaxed him. His eyes and limbs felt heavy and he succumbed to sleep.

The dream took him to the same narrow street. It was dark and mild. There was no sound of a scream, no running feet. It was silent.

Chapter 13

1929

'State your full name please,' said the clerk to the court.

'Captain David Morris.'

'Thank you, you may sit down.' David was glad to sit because his legs felt weak.

The trial began with the prosecution, led by KC Arnold Jones, laying out the case against him. When he got to the attack he placed the blame on David saying he invented a robber. David wanted to shout, 'It wasn't me. I could never do that I loved her.' But he resisted having been warned by Philip Keene that any emotional outburst would alienate the jury and the judge.

Mr Harrison was called to the stand and was asked to talk about the dance at the Royal Hall. It was shocking to see him so frail as if he had shrivelled with grief. His voice quavered and he did not look at David as he spoke. 'My wife and I accompanied our niece, Annabelle, to the dance as chaperones. Captain Morris asked her to dance and then he joined us at our table. He struck me then as a reliable gentleman and when he offered to escort her home, to allow us to leave early, I agreed. It never occurred to me that he would walk her home. I assumed he would call a cab.'

The judge asked Philip if he wanted to ask Mr Harrison any questions but he said he did not. The hatcheck girl at the Royal Hall was then called. She looked scared but managed to say that David had carried a heavy cane with a silver top and left it and his white silk scarf with her. She also confirmed, after collecting his belongings, he had left with Mrs Larkin. This time Philip did have a question.

'Were you able to observe the number of cabs available when Mrs Larkin and Captain Morris were ready to leave?'

'Well I don't have a complete view of the front when I'm behind my counter but most guests had gone so I moved out to get some air. I ran back in as soon as I saw them coming but there were no cabs; they'd all been taken.'

'So they had no choice but to walk.' The girl nodded. There were no more questions so she was allowed to leave the witness box.

The constable who had found Annabelle's body took her place.

'I was walking my beat and I noticed something odd. There was a man kneeling astride a person on the ground. Later I saw the person was a woman. The man appeared to be..... er. His body was going up and down. Forgive me, m' lord, but it looked a bit like a rape.' There was an outbreak of shock from the gallery.

Arnold Jones waited until it had subsided and then said, 'Continue please constable. What action did you take?'

'I shouted, blew me whistle and the assailant disappeared. I felt the woman's pulse but she was dead so I ran back to the station and got the doctor and the undertaker.'

'Thank you constable, no more questions.'

Philip stood and asked, 'Could you explain what you meant when you said the assailant disappeared? Did he run off?'

'It was very strange sir. I saw him, shouted and put my head down to find my whistle. When I went to blow it I saw he'd gone.'

'What was the lighting like? Could you see the man clearly?'

'They were close to a street light and I could see he had no shirt on.'

''Did you see his shirt lying nearby?'

'No sir but there was a wad of something around the lady's head and later it was found to be a sort of shirt.'

'Was it a dress shirt that a gentleman might wear to a dance?'

'No sir it had no collar, buttons or proper stiff cuffs. It had short sleeves and was made of some soft material, perhaps wool; definitely not a smart shirt.'

The judge turned to the prosecution. 'Do we have this shirt as evidence?'

The prosecutor stood to reply. 'Yes sir. I was going to present it during the evidence of the doctor.'

'I think we would all like to see it now, Mr Jones.'

The shirt was held up and there were gasps as the people saw the simple garment, normally blue, stained brown with dried blood. The judge waited until the room became silent and then asked Mr Jones to call his next witness, the doctor.

'Please tell us Doctor Sullivan, about the events of that night.'

'I was called by the police about midnight, or perhaps a bit later, to go to the scene of a crime. When I got there I examined the body of a woman, aged middle thirties, and I pronounced her dead. I examined her in more detail at the morgue and saw she had received a severe blow to the temple on the right hand side.' His hand came up to his own head to show where the blow had struck.

'Had the woman been sexually assaulted?'

'There was no evidence to suggest that.'

'I have no further questions.'

Philip stood up. 'Doctor Sullivan, do you think it possible that the shirt was used by someone to try to stop the bleeding?'

'It is possible, in fact probable.'

'Do you think the shirtless man was attacking Mrs Larkin or could he have been trying to save her?'

'I don't know. I didn't see him.'

'Thank you, no further questions.'

As the doctor moved out of the witness box the judge announced it was lunchtime and a general commotion broke out. David was led down into the cells and lunch was brought to him. He had no appetite and was glad when Robert Finch arrived. His words were kind and he had a brisk, positive air but said he wished they could find the man without the shirt because he may have witnessed the attack.

After lunch Detective Peterson was called to the stand. He was asked to describe, in detail, his investigation.

'We began by examining the scene of the crime and we retrieved Mrs Larkin's evening bag. This contained her ticket to the ball at the Royal Hall, her dance card, handkerchief and powder compact. This was enough for us to identify the victim because her name was on the card. We notified the next of kin, Mr Harrison, and we were going to visit Captain Morris at his house but he came to the station.' He paused giving the prosecution a chance to ask a question.

'Why did you think to contact Captain Morris?'

'His name was on the dance card and we had already informed Mrs Larkin's relatives of her death and they mentioned him by name.'

Philip stood, 'How would you describe the captain's appearance when you first met him, the morning after the tragedy?'

'His head was bandaged and what I could see of his face was bruised.'

'So there was irrefutable evidence that he had been attacked.'

'I could not say that, sir, it is possible to self inflict such wounds or he could have fought with Mrs Larkin.'

Philip sat down. It was not going well. Detective Peterson continued to outline his investigation and, even without a witness to the attack, he seemed to be persuading the jury of his client's guilt. Philip knew he would need to come up with some real evidence tomorrow, but the elusive Good Samaritan had not responded to his advertisements in the newspapers.

The trial ended for the day and David was taken back to a cell. Robert Finch and Philip visited to say comforting words but David felt they were just being kind. The defence would put their case tomorrow and then the jury would make their decision. His life rested in the hands of those people and he felt depressed and resigned.

The gaoler brought him a meal but he was so full of emotion he had difficulty swallowing. Later he closed his eyes and slept until morning.

He woke with a start and found to his surprise that he felt hungry. He ate his breakfast quickly and was glad when it was time to go back into the court. In his mind the outcome was inevitable and he just wanted it all to end.

Philip stood up and addressed the jury.

'Good morning. I know you have listened carefully to the case for the prosecution and many among you may have already made a decision as to the innocence or guilt of Captain Morris. But…..' He paused and let his gaze wander across them. He noticed many looked down a clear sign he would need to sow more than a little seed of doubt in order to win.

'I am going to show that the case for the prosecution is based on no true evidence; it is all circumstantial. They have failed to produce one witness to the crime itself. They have not found a motive of any kind. What did Captain Morris gain from the death of Mrs Larkin? Nothing; he had no reason to do it. Now I am going to call my first witness for the defence, Mr Martin Caruthers.'

Caruthers moved with military bearing into the witness box. He was sworn to tell the truth and then Philip asked him to tell his story about the night of Annabelle's death. David was impressed with his friend and wished he could thank him as he described their friendship and then the events of the night of the attack. David looked at the jury and they seemed to emanate some sympathy for him and for the first time he wondered if there was hope. When Philip had finished the prosecution questioned Caruthers.

'Mr Caruthers, would it be fair to say that you did not actually witness the attack?'

'I think I made that clear in my statement, sir.'

'You also made it clear that Captain Morris was in some distress when he arrived at your home that night. Bleeding from an injury to his head, I understand and you helped him.'

'I did what any friend would do.'

'Thank you Mr Caruthers, I have no further questions.' Caruthers was instructed to leave the witness box and as he moved he glanced over to David who nodded his thanks.

In desperation Philip called David to the stand. David told the truth in a depressed and monotonous tone. He did not look at the jury. It no longer mattered to him now if he lived or died and the latter seemed inevitable.

Philip's closing arguments echoed his opening ones but he knew David's demeanour and lacklustre performance had condemned him. The judge declared it was time for lunch and instructed the jury to return only when they had made their decision. He pointed out that without witnesses to the deed they had a difficult task and to take their time weighing the evidence.

David refused lunch and waited impatiently to go back and hear his fate. It was not very long before everyone was recalled. The Foreman stood to give the verdict. He said just one word, 'guilty'. There was a noisy reaction from the gallery and order had to be restored for the judge to pronounce his sentence. There was total silence when he produced the black cap but immediately he had finished there was uproar and some people cheered. David was hustled out of the court quickly, his legs refusing to obey his need to walk out with dignity.

In the quiet of his cell, shaking with shock, he realised he felt relieved. He wanted it to be over quickly. It was going to be impossible to sleep but he was exhausted. He closed his eyes and awoke with horror to face his last few hours of life.

The prison officers were very kind and brought him a huge cooked breakfast. When he had eaten as much as he could manage a priest visited him. 'I am Father Kinsella, Would you like to confess your sins before you meet your maker?'

'I will not ask forgiveness because I'm innocent and God knows that. I would welcome a prayer, though. The priest recited several prayers and then the prison officers returned and said it was time.

'I will stay with you throughout, my son,' said the priest and the small group walked with him to the scaffold.

David stood on the trap door and heard prayers being intoned as the noose was put around his neck. Whilst he was wondering whether this was really happening the floor gave way and he fell. The jerk broke his neck. His body writhed, spasmed and then swung, limp; he was dead.

Chapter 14

When Phil got home after sailing he felt wretched. How could he have been so rough with Jason who was still struggling with bereavement? Should he ring and apologise? In the end he rang Jenny and asked if they could meet for a drink that evening.

'I thought we didn't meet on Sundays,' she said. 'Sailing takes priority over everything.'

'Please don't get at me, Jen, I need to see you tonight. I know it's a work day tomorrow so just for an hour.' She agreed and they met at eight in their favourite pub.

When they were sipping their drinks in the beer garden Jenny asked why he had asked to see her. 'Is there something wrong?'

'No, not really, I wanted to see you because I was annoyed at Jason after sailing and was unnecessarily harsh.' Phil told her all about it and she nodded with understanding.

'I don't know many people our age who have lost their wives like Jason and I expect the same goes for you.' She was encouraged to go on by Phil's concentration on her every word. 'You feel bad but if this had happened before Catherine died would you have said the same things?'

'Probably. As Jason said I really like to win.'

'Right, so your reaction was totally normal. I think the best way to treat him *is* to be normal. I don't think he would want everyone treading on eggshells, scared of saying anything that might upset him.'

Phil sat back in his chair more relaxed and drank some of his lager. 'I certainly hadn't looked at it that way but now you've said it I think you're right. You've really helped, thank you.'

She smiled and his heart lurched. He knew he was falling in love and was too scared to tell her. It was too early in their relationship. He needed to be sure she felt the same. 'I don't know how you can be so wise as well as beautiful,' he said.

84

'Flattery won't work tonight, Phil, much as I love to hear it. We agreed on just one hour as it's school for me tomorrow but the hour isn't up yet so would you like the same again?'

'That would be great, thanks.'

Jason expected to dream that night so it was no surprise when he found himself in the same alley. He walked slowly towards the light and as he did so he heard a couple chatting, quietly. There was Annabelle, the woman, who had been dead, now alive and vibrant. They looked like a couple from 'Downton Abbey' as if he had stumbled onto a film set. Then, with shocking speed, a man ran up behind them with a cudgel raised to attack. Annabelle screamed as Jason launched himself upon the attacker. She continued to wail and scream, 'David, help! Oh someone help!' as David and Jason fought the assailant. Together they disarmed him and eventually wrestled him to the ground. They had both received a bruise or two from the flailing cudgel but as they held the man face down, breathing heavily they looked at each other and grinned.

They stayed in position as they heard a whistle and a policeman ran up to them and took control. 'Right if you two gents would continue to hold this man down I will get him into handcuffs, then you can explain what happened.'

'We were just standing, talking when he ran up to attack us. David couldn't see him but I screamed and this man,' she pointed to Jason, 'came to our rescue. There was a fight but eventually they got the stick away from him.'

At that moment several other policemen arrived, in response to the whistle, and they took the assailant to the police station.

'I know you must all feel shaken by this attack but I would like you to come to the station now and give a statement each, while it's still fresh in your minds.'

'I'll never forget this. It was such a shock. I couldn't sleep now anyway so I'm happy to come with you officer.' Annabelle spoke with such conviction both Jason and David smiled again and nodded their agreement. Jason led, with the policeman, whilst David and Annabelle followed, his arm around her protectively.

At the station David agreed to give his statement first and was taken into a small room leaving Annabelle and Jason together.

'I cannot thank you enough for your help this evening. I don't know what would have happened if you had not been there. We ought to introduce ourselves. My name's Annabelle Larkin.'

She held out her hand and Jason shook it. 'I'm Jason Brownlow and I'm glad I could be of service to you both.'

'Well, Mr Brownlow, I am forever in your debt. You see that awful man attacked us just as David proposed to me. I told him I wasn't sure I was ready to marry again but now I am. I was so frightened during the fight that he was going to be killed and then it made me realise just how much I love him.'

Before Jason could comment the door opened and David emerged and shook hands with the sergeant who had taken his statement. Annabelle was asked to go in next, leaving Jason and David together.

David thanked Jason, as Annabelle had done, and they exchanged names.

'I must tell you that robber chose his moment very badly for me. I had just asked Mrs Larkin, a widow by the way, to marry me. She didn't refuse me, exactly, and I was intent on persuasion when it happened. I didn't hear his footsteps at all and it could have been serious if you'd not been there.'

'Yes it could have gone badly for you both but everything worked out well. Mrs Larkin did mention your proposal to me whilst you were giving your statement. I hope you will ask her again because she hinted that fearing for your life during the fight made her realise how much she felt for you.'

'She really said that? Thank you for telling me, Mr Brownlow. It's possible the attacker did me a huge favour.'

The door opened and they both stood up as Annabelle came out. She went straight into David's open arms as Jason moved to take her place in the interview room. He thought about the attack and felt deeply satisfied with his night's work and grinned as he realised he had also played Cupid. Surely going back into the past and changing history couldn't be wrong if the outcome felt so good.

The sergeant gestured for Jason to sit down and then said, 'Oh, just one moment sir, I meant to tell the couple they could go home now. Please wait while I do that. They have had more than enough for one night.' Jason nodded settled into his chair and was then overcome by a need to close his eyes. He felt disorientated, nauseous and opened his eyes in alarm.

The interview room was gone and he was on his own bed. He sat up and then lay down again as waves of dizziness swept over him. The timer had brought him home before he could give his statement so there was no written record of his existence in 1929. In its haste it had left him feeling ill.

Daylight was seeping through the curtains so he turned his head to look at the bedside clock. It was almost seven so he needed to get up for work. Perhaps if he moved slowly he could do it. Sitting up still brought some vertigo but it was less than before so he attempted to stand and found he could.

After a shower and breakfast Jason felt normal but very excited. He had promised to phone Sonia before he went to work and dearly wanted to rush around to her house and blurt out the story but something held him back. He picked up the phone.

'Hello, Sonia, as you can hear I'm fine but I've lots to tell you so can you meet me for lunch today? Excellent, I'll see you there at 12. I've got a free period at the beginning of the afternoon so we don't have to eat and run.' She had suggested a restaurant quite close to his school; a perfect choice but now he needed to return, mentally, to the present because it was time to go to work. His sports bag was by the door so he collected it and left the house whistling.

Sonia put the phone down with a sigh. It was partly a sigh of relief that he was safe but also tinged with anxiety. What had happened? What had he done that had made him sound so chirpy? She wished she had someone to talk to who had experience of time travel. If only Dr Who was real.

She was not dressed yet so she selected clothes to make her feel in control, sensible grey trousers, a pretty pink blouse and a light grey linen jacket if it should be cool. As she ate breakfast, cereal with fruit, and sipped her coffee she worked on a Times crossword. It was not going well because she was unable to concentrate. Jason would be out on the field now running around with the youngsters, demonstrating and encouraging. That was what she really needed, some physical activity.

She changed out of her smart, sensible clothes and began to clean the house. There had been other occasions when her world seemed to be moving along without her and manual work had helped. There would be no need to think, just work hard, concentrating on each task and, hopefully, solutions would come to her.

Sonia lived in a ground floor apartment in an elegant Georgian Terrace. The ceilings were high and the rooms generous in size. When cleaning she frequently shut the door on the spare bedroom but today she vacuumed with a will, even pulled out the bed from the wall and cleaned behind it. After dusting she took down the curtains. They were made of cotton with a pretty yellow daisy motif and put them in the washing machine. It was a perfect moment to clean the window and she would then move onto her bedroom and do the same, perhaps not the curtains because they needed dry cleaning.

Sonia worked for an hour and a half and then, pleased with her efforts, made herself a cold drink and sat down with a notepad.

Who would be affected by Jason's change to the past, assuming he had done so?

She wrote.

1.   *Friends, relatives, descendants of Annabelle.*
2.   *Friends, relatives, descendants of Captain Morris.*
3.   *Nathan Morris.*
4.   *What happens to those people when something is changed? Do they go back to before the event and play it over again? Do they notice?*
5.   *Is this happening all the time?*
6.   *Has this anything to do with people recognising places they have never been to - déjà vu?*

She read the list again. It solved nothing but had helped her to focus. It was now time to change and meet Jason so she folded the notepaper and placed it in her handbag.

After a quick wash she dressed in the clothes she had put on earlier and set off to walk to their rendezvous.

It was another lovely early summer's day and she hummed happily as she walked. The anxiety she had felt was lifted and she was ready for whatever he had to tell her.

The café had tables outside so she sat under an umbrella, feeling a little too warm. When the waitress arrived she ordered a cold, dry white wine and sipped it with enjoyment. By the time Jason arrived she felt cooler and relaxed.

'You look very comfortable there, Sonia, but can we eat inside? I don't really want any staff, or even worse pupils, coming up for a chat.'

'No problem,' she said as she collected her bag and picked up what was left of her wine. They sat at a table away from the window and looked at the menu. They both chose a salad but Jason added a side order of chips.

'I haven't had much sleep and it's been a busy morning so I need some carbohydrate. Anyway whilst we wait for that let me tell you about last night.'

He related the story and Sonia listened, enthralled.

When he'd finished she said, 'You've actually met and spoken to people who've been dead for about ninety years. That's incredible.'

'What seems incredible to me is seeing Annabelle so very much alive. The other times I've seen her she was dead. Oh, I forgot to tell you that Annabelle was on Catherine's Family Tree. She was her grandmother's aunt.'

'Whoa, this is all going too fast for me,' said Sonia.

'I'm sorry to have thrown that in so carelessly but I only discovered that last night and saving Annabelle put it out of my mind.'

Sonia frowned as she spoke. 'You met Nathan Morris a short while ago and he told you his grandfather had been hanged for murder. Now you've changed all that.'

'Yes,' said Jason, But I don't know how David Morris died the second time round. I hope he married Annabelle and lived happily ever after.' He looked at Sonia, disturbed by her slow response. 'What's the matter?'

'Has it occurred to you that Nathan Morris may no longer exist? You don't know exactly when he was conceived.'

'My God, could I have deprived him of his life? I must ring the prison.'

Their lunch arrived and Jason, awed by the possible consequences of changing the past, felt his hunger diminish. He toyed with a chip as Sonia reached for her bag and showed him her list.

'I think we must do some research,' she said. 'Perhaps we can find the answers to these questions. I also think you should handle that timer with gloved hands and take it to the tip. You seem to have done what it wanted and now it must go.' Jason nodded and began to eat with some appreciation.

'Shall I go to the library and see if I can find out anything whilst you're at work this afternoon?'

Jason looked at his watch. 'That would be great. Give me a ring or a text if you have any success. I've got to go now and, no argument, I'll pay the bill at the counter. Thanks for everything Sonia.'

He kissed her and left.

Sonia finished her second glass of wine and walked towards the library. It seemed the right place to go but then she realised Somerset House would have what she needed. They had records of all births, deaths and marriages but it meant going to London. She turned on her heel, went home and packed an overnight bag. She phoned for a taxi to take her to the station and rang Somerset House and asked if she needed an appointment to search for records. She was told, to her surprise, that they no longer had public records. These were now held in the Public Records Office in Myddleton Street and also Kew.

I should have done some research before rushing to London, she thought, but it seemed the office in Kew was where people went to research their family trees.

The taxi arrived and the journey to the station took just ten minutes. She bought her ticket and sat in the sunshine waiting for the train. Kew gardens would be lovely to visit after her research, she thought, so she used her smart phone to find a hotel near there. The train arrived and she found her seat and relaxed into it. As it pulled away she sent a text to Jason, explaining her actions and one to Roger. She closed her eyes and fell asleep lulled by the gentle movement of the carriage.

Chapter 15

Sports day was imminent so Jason worked hard that afternoon encouraging reluctant teenagers to enter races. He stayed late after school and became totally engrossed with the programme for it, updating the one from last year. Saving Annabelle had left him with a feeling of closure and he was able to concentrate without interruption. Finally he sat back with a sigh of contentment and Sonia came into his mind. Had she discovered anything?

He collected his bag from the locker and took out his phone. There was a text from her. She was in London to do his research in the Public Records Office. He felt guilty when he realised how seriously she took his actions of the night before and decided to ring her when he got home. The traffic noise was too great where he was and he needed quiet to think. He could also access Catherine's memory stick. He quickened his pace and eventually broke into a jog. It felt good to be running again, even if his bag encumbered him. By the time he got home his mood had lightened.

He made a cup of tea, took it into his den and put the computer on. While it was starting up he rang Sonia.

'Sonia! I can't believe you've shot off to London. You never mentioned this at lunch time.'

'No, well I didn't think of it then. Anyway it may have been a bit impetuous but then that's me all over. I much prefer action to thinking things through. Anyway I have nothing to report because I've just settled into my hotel and I will start tomorrow. In fact I can't chat for long Jason because I'm meeting Roger off the train and then we're going out to dinner.'

'I thought Roger lived up here.'

'He does but I texted him that I was popping off to London and he decided to join me.'

'Well, that's nice. You'll have to introduce me to Roger sometime. I think he must be smitten.'

'I don't know how smitten he is but I really like him. We have fun and laugh a lot. I'll invite you round to meet him when I get back. Well I must fly, bye Jason.' The phone went dead and he hadn't even had time to say goodbye.

He put the memory stick into the computer and opened Catherine's family tree. There was Annabelle and he was shaken to see a second marriage to Captain David Morris dated May 1930. He imagined them both, so happy. They died within six months of each other, having had thirty years of marriage. There were no children listed and that line of the family ended there. He wanted to tell Sonia but it could wait. She would find it out for herself anyway.

He looked at the family tree again and scrolled along it to see how far back it went. 1852 there was a Lord Marshall. He had a son, George and a daughter, Jane. Jane had married but her husband had died in India.

Jason sat back, his eyes staring at the screen but not seeing it. He was back in the auction room and realised he had been into Marshall Hall before, in a dream. This was the home of one of Catherine's relations. The woman, looking so sad, sitting by the fire was, almost certainly Jane. She was caressing a dog and dressed in black; recently widowed? When did he dream that? It was the day he'd bought the timer.

He remembered an overwhelming desire to help the woman but he was powerless looking at her through glass. Knowing the power of the timer he realised that feeling of frustration was not his, but its. The timer was trapped in a cupboard, not being touched and was powerless to help.

Sonia had said the timer had to go and he knew she was right. It had taken over his life for weeks and he needed to take back control. Who knew what mission the timer might send him on next? Would he find himself helping Jane Marshall or was there another relative? There were too many possible changes to the past that affect the present.

He needed some sanity so he rang Phil.

'Hi Jason. Are you ringing to confirm Sunday, 'cause I'm just off out with Jenny. I'm taking her for an Indian.'

'Er, no, I was actually ringing to cancel Sunday. The long range forecast shows it to be very quiet, no more than a force two so I thought I'd go to see my Dad. Really neglected him and feel guilty.'

'Oh, well that might be a good thing for me too. Jenny's been nagging that every Sunday is sailing and we never get time to do anything together. We can make plans tonight. Right, gotta go, see ya.'

Phil rang off and Jason realised he was feeling envious. Phil and Jenny had become an item and he was glad for them both but it made him miss Catherine all the more.

Dad was pleased he'd rung and said he would cook them a steak dinner and maybe apple pie and custard but he would buy the pie, Jason offered to bring the apple pie and arranged to get there at midday. He put the phone down and felt his stomach gurgling. It was all that talk about food.

He shut down the computer and went into the kitchen. His fridge had some mature cheddar and eggs so he could make an omelette but he wrinkled his nose. The Indian sounded good, so he rang and ordered a take away. There was a wait of half an hour. In that time he could write a list of things to do tomorrow.

Ring Armley Gaol
Dispose of timer
Buy frozen/fresh apple pie for Sunday
Print 500 copies of Sports Day programme
Talk to Jenny about field layout for S.D.

He paused and then his eyes rested on the second item. How? He could wrap it in bubble wrap and take it to a charity shop. Was that fair? Another person could buy it and become embroiled in excursions to the past. Should he take it to the tip as Sonia had suggested? No, he couldn't bring himself to do that. It was such a lovely object and meant no harm, only good. But it had to go, somehow.

He stood up, donned thick gloves, wrapped the timer in bubble wrap and placed it in a plastic bag. Indecisive for a moment he then took the bag into the garage.

He looked at his watch, grabbed his wallet, and keys and drove to collect his Indian meal.

It was lunchtime the following day before Jason was free to ring the prison and he was shocked to find they had never had an inmate called Nathan Morris. He asked if they had a record of his visit and they said not. He stood for a moment, thinking. How could he clearly remember going to see Nathan? Sonia remembered too. Why hadn't their memories been expunged? Perhaps changes made to the past only affect those directly involved. Nathan had said he had brothers but if Nathan's father did not exist nor did his brothers, unless they were by different fathers.

The timer wanted him to help Annabelle and it had felt good when he did but how many lives had been changed by his actions? What about all the people who knew Nathan and his brothers? What about Nathan's mother?

Lunch hour was almost over so he opened his sandwiches and ate them, without relish. He needed to focus on school and the afternoon's athletics. It was nearly the end of term and Sports Day was tomorrow.

The afternoon passed quickly and after school he went to the office to collect his set of programmes. Everything was organised now so he could go home and the first thing he would do was ring Sonia.

He opened the front door and a thought struck him. If Annabelle didn't die then he didn't leave his pyjama top at the crime scene. He went straight up stairs and found it in the washing bin. There were no bloodstains. It was spooky, but everything that had happened since his first dream was spooky. He looked for the pillowcase that he had cut up for analysis. It was also in the washing bin, completely whole. Would Phil remember testing it? He clung to Sonia's premise that the timer was benign and hoped she was right. Still thinking about Sonia he went downstairs just as she rang him.

'Hi Jason we're having a lovely time and have decided to extend our stay and take in a show. Roger has never seen Les Mis' so we've booked it for tomorrow night.'

'Excellent. I'm really glad you're enjoying yourselves. Did you do any research?'

'Yes. There was no record of a Nathan Morris and I wondered if you'd called Armley Gaol.'

'Yes and they've never heard of him, or my visit. Nathan had brothers. Did you find anything about them?'

'No. The line from your Captain David Morris died with him because he and Annabelle had no children. We don't know Nathan's mother's name so we can't take this any further. Have you dumped the timer?'

'Sort of.'

'What's that mean? Listen Jason; by the time I get home I want it gone. It's too powerful. Who knows what it might do next?'

'Ok, I will. Have a great time and enjoy the show. Bye Sonia.'

Sonia put down the phone and changed for dinner. Roger may not have seen many London shows but he knew all the best restaurants and tonight they were going to one owned by a Celebrity Chef.

Sonia loved the whole ambience of dining out in style and had bought a dress with a toning jacket for the occasion. She had also bought extra underwear, and a light daytime outfit. When she had set out for London she had only bought enough to stay overnight so extending the visit had been expensive, but delightful. Everything was delightful, she thought, and knew that she was totally hooked on Roger. He was such good company and they laughed so much.

They took a taxi to Soho and went to a seafood restaurant. When they were shown to their table Roger ordered a bottle of vintage champagne.

'Are we celebrating something?' she asked.

'I hope so. I feel like celebrating every time I see you.'

'That's a lovely thing to say, Roger, and I do love champagne.'
He put his hand out across the table and she took it.

'Sonia. Will you marry me? I live for the times I see you and the more I do the less I want to go back to my lonely house. I desperately want to be with you all the time. What do you say?'

Before she could answer the champagne arrived. They dropped hands as the waiter popped the cork and went through the tasting ritual. When the waiter moved away Sonia picked up her glass, clinked his and said, 'I'd love to marry you Roger. So this is an engagement party. I think you should kiss me.' They stood, moved around the table and he took her in his arms. The kiss was long and passionate. They were oblivious to the other diners and Sonia thought she had never been so happy.

Chapter 16

2016

Sports Day dawned sunny with a cool breeze that meant it was perfect for athletics. The PA system worked and the races followed each other efficiently. The recorders managed to keep abreast of everything and by the end of the day the chair of governors handed out medals and a shield for the house that had won the most points.

Finally the head quietly congratulated Jason on a successful event. Jenny bubbled with excitement when she heard that and said, 'Let's go for a drink before going home.'

'Excellent idea, the Pitcher and Piano?'

'Great, I'll meet you there in about half an hour, so I can shower and change.'

The bar was not busy and Jason arrived before Jenny and ordered a pint of lager. He was half way down it when she arrived and he looked approvingly at her lithe figure. Phil was a lucky man. He hoped he appreciated what he had.

'What would you like to drink to celebrate a brilliant Sports Day?' She grinned, 'A glass of Prosecco, please. Somehow it seems more of a celebration if the wine has some fizz.'

Jason bought a large glass and two packets of crisps and brought them back to the table. When he had settled into his seat, Jenny held up her glass. 'Here's to many more, perfectly choreographed, Sports Days.'

'I'll drink to that.' They clinked glasses and smiled at each other.

Jason removed her smile with an innocent question. 'How are you and Phil getting on? I understand you're going to do something lovely on Sunday as we're not sailing.'

'Actually we've had a row so I'm not sure about Sunday at the moment.'

'Oh, I'm sorry, I was just thinking earlier he was a lucky man to have you.'

She grimaced. 'It's not him it's me. I'm the one who wants to take it slower and its all your fault.'

'Mine? What have I done?'

She wriggled in her seat. 'Sorry, I shouldn't have said that especially as we're celebrating.'

'You're going to have to explain, Jenny. You can't leave it like that. I don't understand what I've done to affect your relationship but I'll put it right if I can. This is going to sound really corny but friendships and love are vital. I've only realised that so much since Catherine died.'

She put out a hand to touch his arm. 'So there you have it. There's nothing you can do to help. I've watched the devastating effect Catherine's death has had on you and I'm scared of that. I don't want to fall in love and be hurt. It's so cruel and painful.'

'No, you can't think like that. Catherine was the best thing that ever happened to me and I value every moment we had. Yes, it was cruel when she had the accident but I don't regret loving her. If you have deep feelings for Phil let them blossom into love. Take the risk of being hurt. It's worth it.' He looked into her eyes and saw she was crying.

She stood abruptly, 'Just going to the ladies.'

Jason downed his pint and bought a second before Jenny returned. She was smiling, ruefully. 'I'm sorry, Jason. I've calmed down now and I'll finish my drink. She glugged it down and jumped up. I'm going to get another. Are you OK or shall I get you one?'

'No, I'm fine, thanks.' He drank some more and finished his crisps whilst he waited wondering if he'd helped her at all.

'Right,' she said sitting back down with him,' Thank you for saying what you did. It's really helped me to focus. I'm going to ring Phil tonight and, hopefully, make arrangements for Sunday.'

'Good. I've never been a matchmaker but I think I might have just qualified.' They both smiled and the conversation returned to the safe topic of Sports day]. Jenny remarked on a pupil that excelled her expectations and both of them laughed at little incidents they remembered.

When he got home Jason decided he would go for a run in the morning and fit another in on Sunday morning before he went to see his dad. He found his iPod, intending to run to music. Sometimes it was good to let the music and the rhythm of running take over. If he just ran his thoughts would interfere. He thought of Sonia and Roger having a lovely weekend in London and had to quell more jealous thoughts. He must focus on his fitness.

The next morning he set off, feet pounding the pavement in time with the music. He was mindlessly active, his arms pumping as well as his legs but stopped abruptly when he realised he'd taken a different route. He was near the doctors at the road junction where Catherine had died. His breathing was laboured and it was not all the exertion of running. Tears ran down his face. How could he have run to this place when he'd been avoiding it for months? He turned away and walked for a while, confused and bereft then made the effort to run again, trying to shake off the threatening depression.

Back home he made a shopping list and decided to clean all the windows inside and out. Losing himself in activity raised his mood and when he entered the supermarket he was able to concentrate and filled his trolley with healthy food for the following week. He also remembered to buy an apple pie and a bottle of Malbec to take to his Dad's.

The following day he left his iPod at home determined to concentrate as he ran so he would not veer from his usual route. Thoughts crowded into his mind. The adventures he'd had with the timer had helped him cope with losing Catherine and now it was over he felt vulnerable, less confident. It had also brought him much closer to Sonia and she had helped him too. He mused in this vein for a while then stopped running with a jerk. He had taken the same route as yesterday. Now he felt scared.

I must talk to Sonia, he thought, convinced he was being controlled and the only culprit had to be the timer. I'll meet her at lunchtime on Monday, if she can make it, but I know what she'll say. I must take the timer to the tip and throw it deep into a skip. I still want to see her. I can't talk to Dad about this.

Dad opened the door, and his arms. The hug filled Jason with the warmth and security he'd felt as a child.

'There's a lovely smell of roast beef. I can't wait.'

'Well you'll have to because it wont be ready for an hour but that gives us time to open that wine and have a pre-dinner drink, or would you prefer coffee?'

'I've had a coffee and the wine sounds good. I'll open it.' Jason went into the familiar kitchen that still seemed empty without Mum. He quelled that thought, knowing he was feeling vulnerable to emotions today. Perhaps the wine wasn't such a good idea. It could make him maudlin. As this thought went through his mind he screwed the corkscrew deep into the cork and pulled down the arms. The cork obediently rose and he wiggled it out. He carried the two glasses into the living room and sat opposite Dad.

'Cheers,' Dad said and sipped it. 'That's really good, fruity and no oaky tang. Thanks Jason.'

'It was Jenny put me onto to it and now I always keep a bottle or two at home.'

'Do I know Jenny? Have you got a girlfriend?'

'No and No. Sorry, Jenny is a member of staff who helps part time in my department. She is also going out with my sailing buddy, Phil.'

Dad nodded,' I know Phil.

Jason went on to chat about sailing and Sports Day, and then it was time to eat. Dad carved the beef, succulent and pink in the middle, and Jason ate some before it reached the plate.

'You used to do that as a boy and Mum would tell you off.'

They both smiled at the memory and busied themselves loading the plates with vegetables, Yorkshire pudding and thick gravy. It was delicious and Jason wondered if he'd be able to eat any of the apple pie, now warming in the oven.

'Shall we clear up and load the dishwasher before pud? I might be able to eat it if we have a break,' he said.

'No leave it for me to do when you've gone home. Let's sit in a comfy chair and I'll tell you about the Tuesday Club.'

'Tuesday Club?' Jason knew nothing about it and realised he should visit Dad more often.

'We meet every week both men and women. Sometimes we have a speaker and other times it's a trip out or we play board games. We always have tea and biscuits or cake and a raffle. I enjoy it, chatting to new people and making friends.'

'That sounds great, have you seen any of those new friends in between?'

'Well, I've seen Joan a few times. She goes to short mat bowls on a Thursday morning and invited me to come. I went along and had a go. It's not at all straightforward. You watch it on the telly and those balls curve gracefully towards the white but not mine. They curved in all the wrong places at first but I began to get the hang of it the second time and now I partner Joan and we do quite well.'

Jason was delighted and amazed at this new, gregarious Dad.

'You see, I needed to fill the hole in my life when Mum died and this year was even bleaker with Catherine going. I was getting depressed so I pulled myself up and decided I needed to join things. My life is fuller now and I really look forward to going to my activities. It's different for you, working all week and then sailing. Your life is already full of activity. Anyway I'm ready for that pie now.'

He sprang out of the chair and into the kitchen leaving Jason, full of admiration.

'Do you want some help with the custard?'

'No, lad, I got a carton so it just needs warming through. Stay there and I'll bring it in shortly.'

Jason went home later that afternoon feeling thoughtful. Dad was right about his active life but he still felt lonely and bereft.

That evening he rang Sonia and asked to meet her, as before at lunchtime. She sounded bubbly and happy and he found himself smiling as he put the phone down. She said she had something to tell him but she wanted to tell him face to face. He couldn't think what it was and hoped he wouldn't spoil her mood by talking about his run.

Chapter 17

'Roger and I are engaged! He popped the question in London and I said yes.'

'Wow, that's fantastic. I'm so pleased for you.' Jason leant over and kissed her cheek. 'So when's the happy day?'

'Oh we haven't got that far. First he's got to tell his family. I haven't even met his son and daughter. They're adults of course but I really need them to like me.'

'They'll love you. Don't worry.'

'I hope so. Anyway we had a wonderful few days in London but I'm afraid I only went to the records office once so I haven't found out anything else. What about you? Did you find out any more?'

Jason told her about the change in Catherine's family tree and her earliest relative, Jane Carstairs (nee Marshall). He said he had not mentioned dreaming of her before because he didn't realise it was anything to do with the timer. He also said he'd found his pyjama top in the washing bin no longer stained with blood. Finally he told her about running to the place where Catherine died.

'It really spooked me and I know it was the timer controlling me.'

Sonia looked up sharply. 'I thought you agreed to get rid of it. You haven't have you?'

Jason sighed. 'Not entirely, I wore thick gloves, wrapped it up and put it in the garage. I hoped that would stop it but obviously not. There was something else too. I don't have any of your psychic sensitivity but I felt the timer didn't want to go.'

Anyone else might have looked askance at this comment but Sonia just nodded. 'Shall I take it to my house? I still believe it's benign. Perhaps it still has a mission to perform.'

'If you believe that I don't think you should take it. What would Roger say if you suddenly disappeared in the middle of the night?'

Sonia laughed and her cheeks went red. 'Well, Roger isn't living with me at the moment but you do have a point.' She frowned. 'I'm not sure what to say. No, that's not true. I have thought of something but I'm reluctant to say it.'

She took a deep breath. 'I think the timer wants you to save Catherine. We know that it's possible, and I'm sure you would want to try. But think about it first, Jason. What's happened since she died? You saved Captain Morris's life. If you turn back the clock you will probably find all that work undone, Nathan still alive and in prison.... and,' she paused and whispered, 'I wouldn't be engaged to my gorgeous Roger.' Her voice tailed off to a whimper but Jason failed to absorb anything she'd said after her first statement.

'I'd do anything to have her back. I don't care what effect it has on recent events. I just think about the devastation losing her meant to me, to you, to her parents and her other friends. I'm incomplete without her, Sonia. I have to try.'

He looked directly at her as he said this and saw tears brimming and then sliding down her cheeks.

'Oh Sonia, I'm sorry, please forgive me. You met Roger on a cruise didn't you?' She nodded, dabbing her eyes and sniffing. 'That was booked before Catherine died wasn't it? So if we go back that much time you will meet him again. Please Sonia. I need your support. I know you came full of delight and I'm spoiling it, but if you love Roger you'll understand how I feel about Catherine.'

The hanky came out again and muffled her voice. 'Of course I understand. I love Catherine too but it just feels I'm about to lose Roger. What a mess.'

The enjoyment of the morning was spoiled and Sonia stood up to leave. Jason went to hug her but she pulled away.

'I'm going home now. Do whatever you need to do. If it works and you prevent Catherine's accident we'll all be catapulted back and won't remember any of this.' She moved towards the door but Jason stopped her.

'I'd like to think that's true. But I still remember visiting Nathan Morris even though he doesn't exist. I thought it might be because I wasn't close to him. But it might be because I'm the one changing things.'

'I remember you going to see him too perhaps because I was your confidante. If I could remember Roger when I meet him on the ship I would make a point of charming him. Anyway, I must go now. Tell me if you have a dream and what happens. Bye Jason.'

Sonia walked quickly home feeling deflated and miserable. She needed to see Roger. She wanted to hold him close, frightened of losing him. How much time did they have left? Chatting to him on the phone raised her spirits and he happily agreed to come over for dinner that evening.

They had arranged previously to meet on Sunday and make the journey to see his daughter, Linda, who had invited them to lunch. Sonia was anxious about meeting his family but appreciated that Linda probably felt the same.

Roger said he would be over at seven and that gave her time to get ready. Rifling through her recipe books she chose a delicious lamb tagine that she had never made for him. It went well with minted couscous and she could make a fruit salad to follow. She moved a bottle of red wine into the dining room to warm and then drove to the supermarket.

An hour later, she picked two full bags out of the car and carried them into the kitchen. She unpacked them and would normally have made a cup of tea and sat reading for a while. This was impossible. She felt so agitated she needed to keep active. Cooking, that's what she would do, prepare the dinner as much as possible in advance and make some shortbread to go with the fruit salad.

As she worked her brain was full of questions. Would Roger recognise her, somehow, if she was shot back in time? Supposing he found a different woman on the cruise. Would she be able to steer things in the right direction? Would she give the game away by knowing something about him that he hadn't told her? Would she remember him at all?

Eventually she made that cup of tea, sat down exhausted, and fell into a troubled sleep. In her dream she had the timer. It took her back to the cruise where she met Roger all over again but he failed to be impressed by her. She wore her most alluring dresses, was vivacious, laughed at his jokes. They made love every night and then, at the end of the holiday, he refused to exchange contact details calling it a shipboard romance that meant absolutely nothing. The dream was a nightmare and she woke with tears filling her eyes.

Once fully awake she looked at the clock and leapt to her feet. It was nearly six thirty and she needed to put finishing touches to the meal, set the table, and change. When she looked in her wardrobe her hand rested on one of the dresses in her dream. She chose, instead, a short cream skirt with a pretty flowery top and finished the effect with sparkling earrings.

When Roger arrived she was looking fresh, attractive and in control. He had no idea of her inner turmoil and she could never have explained it to him.

'You look good enough to eat.'

She smiled, 'If you eat me you won't have room for my lamb tagine and that would be a waste. Would you like a whisky before I dish up?'

'I'd like you, but I'll settle for a whisky. Do you want any help?'

'No, but you can keep me company in the kitchen. She sipped her wine, checked the oven and then put her arms around him.

'I do love you and I can't wait to be Mrs Roger Dutton. Shall we fix a date soon, once I've met Linda and her family?'

He chuckled. 'With you in this mood perhaps dinner could wait. Could it?' She nodded and he drained his whisky, picked her up, and carried her to the bedroom with her giggling in his arms.'

Chapter 18

After his lunch with Sonia Jason walked back to work in a thoughtful mood. He was going to use the timer again, but not sure when to do it. Perhaps he should wait until the weekend, then he grinned as he realised school broke up on Wednesday so he could do it then.

The afternoon was easy with pupils playing cricket or rounders and he just stood checking all was going well, with no arguments.

When he got home he made a ham and cheese omelette and ate it on his lap, watching television.

Normally he looked forward to the end of term, the final assembly and the oldest pupils, full of teenage emotion, coming to say goodbye. Now he just wanted to rush it through.

It was difficult to concentrate on the programme he was watching so he turned it off, and decided to go to bed early and read.

Tuesday, at school was better than he thought and on Wednesday they finished an hour early.

When he got home he felt restless with excitement. He didn't want to wait until he went to bed. Was it possible to use the timer during the day?

He retrieved it from its hiding place, unwrapped it, turned it upside down and placed it back on the shelf in the study. If he wanted to prevent Catherine's accident he would need to turn it again. Perhaps he should wait for the sand to run through. He needed a strenuous activity to fill in the time and as he thought that he looked out at the back garden. The grass was long and cutting it was just what he needed.

He pulled the mower out of the shed, put the cutter to short, so it made him work extra hard and began to push it. The work was energetic and he got hot but refused to allow himself to stop and have a drink until it was done. He downed a glass of water and then brushed the cuttings off the mower and put it away. Then he swept grass off the path and felt a wave of satisfaction and excitement. It occurred to him, as he entered the back door and paused to look back at the tidy lawn that his effort had probably been wasted, if he went back in time.

It was six o'clock and he was feeling hungry so he made a tuna sandwich and took it into the den. He turned the timer over and watched the sand dribble through. 'Please help me to save Catherine,' he whispered and then sat in the armchair and ate without really tasting it. Habit, more than need, drove him to get up and make a cup of tea and then he decided to take it into the lounge, stretch out on the settee, and watch something totally banal on television.

He felt tired, closed his eyes, but his sleep was quickly interrupted.

Catherine was standing in the hallway, looking beautiful and saying, 'I'll only be half an hour.'

'That's half an hour with out your company. I'll drive you,' said Jason.

'What's happened to you today?'

'I'm a reformed character. Today I will chauffeur you. Madam can sit back and enjoy the ride. He opened the door, shepherded her out, and made an ostentatious show of opening the car door. Catherine giggled and sat in the passenger's seat. Jason shut her door and went around the other side and sat behind the wheel.

'Where to madam?'

'You know I'm going to the Well Woman Clinic, so the doctors surgery.'

Jason set off and asked what she was going to have done.

'I'm not really sure. I've never been before but I expect they'll take my blood pressure, check blood sugar, weigh me. It's a really good idea.'

'It is. Do they do a Well Man's Clinic?'

'I don't know. I'll ask but I don't think you need to worry. You're as fit as a fiddle.' They had arrived and she laughed as she opened the door. Isn't that a daft saying? Why would a fiddle be fit?'

He got out of the car and she looked enquiringly at him. 'You don't have to come and hold my hand.'

'I know but I could wait in the surgery or even jog around the car park.'

'Jogging's not a good idea; it's far too slippery. They really should have put salt down on this path.'

'Hold my arm, Madam and I will escort you,' said Jason, reverting to chauffer mode.

'You are in a strange mood. Perhaps you've got the Christmas spirit.'

'Not a drop has touched my lips, I promise.'

Jason sat down in the surgery and looked at his watch. It was 10.45 and Catherine died at 11.05. He stood up, walked to the notice board, read everything there, but took none of it in. He looked at his watch again and only three minutes had gone by. He sighed with anxiety.

Doctor Masterson put his head around the door and asked for his next patient and a young woman with a fractious baby hurried to her appointment. People coughed and shuffled, waiting, as he was. The room felt stuffy, the windows translucent with condensation. He had to get out into the fresh air.

Jason paced, carefully, around the car park shivering in the cold and looked at his watch again, ten fifty-eight. He hadn't saved her yet. What could he do to make sure she survived? At that moment she emerged, smiling. He moved towards her as quickly as he could on the slippery path and hugged her. As he did so he heard the Church clock strike eleven. She had just five minutes to live.

'Let me go Jason.' Her voice was muffled with her face squashed against his chest.

'I never want to let you go, I love you so much,' he said as he released her. She looked up at him with a radiant smile. 'I'm pleased you love me so much because I have some news for you. We're going to have a baby. I told you I was going to a clinic but it was a maternity one. I've had my first scan, look.'

She held out a black and white photograph clearly showing a baby, curled with knees bent and tiny arms. Jason took it, examining every detail feeling tears running down his face. He hugged her again. 'I'm going to be a dad. I can't believe it. Is it a boy or a girl? Did they tell you?'

'I said I didn't want to know. We'll wait and see. Is that ok with you? If not we can find out at the next scan.'

'I'm happy to wait. When will he or she arrive?'

'July the thirtieth so we've plenty of time to get ready.'

Jason looked at his watch. It was ten past eleven. A surge of elation flooded through him.

'What have we got for dinner tonight?'

'I thought we'd have something simple like ham omelette and salad.'

'Forget it. Let's see if we can book a table at that new Bistro and celebrate.'

They drove home, Jason booked the table then Catherine took the phone off him and began a round of calls, telling family and friends their news. That gave him a moment to himself so he went into the study to look for the timer. It was still in the cabinet. He switched on the computer, used Catherine's memory stick and read that Annabelle Larkin had married Captain David Morris. The changes he had wrought were still there.

He had changed their lives and they, presumably, never realised his intervention. Was he asleep now or awake? If this was a dream he never wanted to leave it. He could recall everything that had happened on this day in December and the eight months after that. Had Sonia gone back to December? Was she on her cruise? He wanted to talk to her and ask if she also remembered all that had happened. It occurred to him to text her but as his hand closed over his mobile Catherine called him. He closed the computer down and found her in the lounge.

'I think I've told everyone. I'm almost drunk with congratulations.'

'If you're feeling drunk perhaps we should celebrate in bed.' She wiggled up to him and undid her bra through her clothes.

'I'm game any time.'

They ran upstairs, laughing and made love. It was not just sex. It was a deep expression of their love and joy. Relaxing afterwards enjoying a delicious sense of well being Jason looked at his watch and abruptly sat up. 'Come on, we must get ready for our dinner.'

They washed and dressed as quickly as possible arriving at the restaurant exactly on time.

Sonia awoke feeling queasy. She was in bed, in her cabin aboard the cruise ship and tears filled her eyes as she realised what had happened. Jason must have saved Catherine and she had to begin her relationship with Roger all over again. So this must be the day before Christmas Eve. What was the current time? What was happening today?

She sat up carefully, feeling dizzy but as the room stilled she ventured to stand. The ship's newsletters were on the dressing table so she collected them and her phone and sat in the armchair. Her phone confirmed it was 7.15 in the morning of December the 23rd 2015. She opened the current newsletter and discovered it was to be a day at sea. What had she done already? Had she made any plans with Roger for meeting him? She wanted to scream with frustration and misery. She looked at the previous day's newsletter and saw there had been the trip to the Falkland Islands. She clearly remembered that delightful adventure and found herself smiling at the memory. Yes, they'd agreed to meet for lunch at the Café Marseilles the following day, so that was today. Well at least she knew what they had done and just needed now to be careful what she said.

It was a more positive Sonia that went up to the buffet breakfast an hour later.

She filled her tray with healthy options, remembering that on her return last time she had gained seven pounds, and wandered around looking for somewhere to sit. The American woman who had not really enjoyed the Land Rover trip was on her own so she joined her.

'Hello, Grace, can I share your table?'

'Sure, honey, but I'm not staying much longer because I'm going to the port lecture at ten thirty.'

110

'Well we can chat until you need to leave.' Sonia sipped her coffee and began her plate of fruit. 'The tea was lovely at the WI yesterday, wasn't it?'

Grace grimaced. 'It was the only good thing about the trip. I suppose the penguins were cute but getting there was torture. You were with someone weren't you? Your husband?'

'Oh, no we're not married. We met on board and, so far, we've been enjoying each other's company.'

Grace stood up. 'Well I have to go now but hang on to him. I thought he was something special.' She threaded her way through the tables, wiggling as she went and Sonia felt uncomfortable. It was obvious that if Grace thought Roger special then so could many other women on board. She finished her breakfast and went for a walk around deck seven.

It was windy and when she got to the prow it was all she could do to keep upright but once around that point she was blown along making the walk easier. After eight circuits she was thinking of finding a seat out of the wind to read her book, when she heard her name being called. She stopped and turned, as Roger reached her. 'Well you've certainly had a pace on. I was trying to catch you up, without breaking into a run and had to really work at it.'

'Roger, how lovely.' Sonia smiled with sheer delight.

'It's not quite lunchtime but we could have a drink, coffee or something stronger. What do you think?'

Roger seemed anxious for her company and Sonia was more than happy to have his. 'Oh I think a glass of Chardonnay would set me up for lunch and I've had enough of this breeze.'

He held out his hand, she took it and as they went into the warmth of the ship she felt a surge of happiness.

As they sat, looking at the menu Jason asked, casually, if Catherine had phoned Sonia.

'No, not yet, she's still on her cruise. That's one friend I'd rather tell face to face. Shall we invite her round for a meal when she gets back?'

'Yes, I like Sonia too. You must ask her if she wants to bring a friend.' Catherine nodded. 'I will but I don't think she has anyone special at the moment.'

'Perhaps she'll have met an eligible bachelor on board the ship.' She raised her eyebrows and he responded with a grin.

'We'll have to wait and see,' said Jason.

Part 2

Chapter 19

Eighteen years later, July 2033

Isabelle applied lipstick and looked at herself in the full-length mirror, critically. Should she have straightened her hair? No she liked the auburn, wayward curls reaching just below her shoulders. The slightly messy look suited her, she thought. The dress was flattering but Dad would probably say it was too short. Anyway there was no time to change anything now.

'Are you ready Izzy? 'Cos, Dad's sitting in the car revving up?'

'Yes, coming,' she said grabbing her clutch bag and running down the stairs, passing Mum, out of the front door and pausing only to open the car door and slide in. Mum locked the front door and followed her.

Dad concentrated on pulling out into the traffic before saying, 'You both look lovely but we've barely time to get there now. The birthday girl should really arrive before the first guests turn up.'

'Sorry, Dad, but the Commodore's opening up and the caterers should have been setting up for the last hour. It'll be fine.'

That was followed by a sceptical grunt from Jason who hated to be late.

The anxiety was unnecessary because they arrived at the sailing club before any guests and everything was organised. The tray of welcome drinks was ready near the door and balloons, the centrepiece of each table, swayed and bobbed in the breeze coming through the open windows. At the back of the hall was a 'Happy 18th Birthday ' banner and the trestle tables were laid ready for the meal with colourful cloths strewn with foil eighteens.

'It all looks fantastic. Thank you. Who'd have thought our simple club room could look so good, ' said Izzy. They were still smiling when the first guests arrived, Phil, Jenny and their son Mark. Mark, just fifteen, was holding the present and pushed it at Izzy going red as he did so.

'Thank you, Mark, and everyone. I'll open it later because more people are coming in. There's sparkling wine or orange juice. Speak to you later.'

She placed the present down, turned back and her smile became even broader. 'Aunty Sonia, Uncle Roger; it's been ages.' She hugged them both, took the proffered present and card with thanks and placed it with the other one as more friends and relations arrived.

The meal began when everyone was there and the loud buzz of conversation gave way to the clatter of cutlery on plates and appreciative noises.

When the time came to cut the cake, made by Mum, Dad stood up and tapped the table with a spoon. Everyone looked towards him. 'Thank you all for coming and helping us celebrate Isabelle's special birthday. She's going to cut the cake now.'

Mum and Izzy moved to the cake and Izzy paused whilst there was a flurry of guests wielding mobile phones, then she smiled and pushed the knife into the icing. Everyone clapped and cheered. One of the caterers took the cake into the kitchen to cut it into taster size pieces and then somebody shouted, 'Speech, Izzy, speech.'

In the expectant quiet she looked at all her friends, some from school and others from the sailing club. Her eyes roamed over Mum and Dad's friends that she had known all her life and lingered, finally on Granddad as she spoke.

'It's been a brilliant birthday and I must thank Mum and Dad for organising all this'. When the applause quietened she continued. 'I'd also like to thank, 'Good Food Catering', for that delicious meal,' and she paused again to allow the appreciative whistles and claps. 'Finally I want to thank all of you for coming this evening and for your presents. Now I would like you to push the tables to each side so we've room to dance because I think our DJ, Rick, is ready. Rick gave a thumbs-up and his music began to a flurry of willing people moving tables and chairs.

Two hours later, as the last guest left, Izzy, Mum and Dad began clearing up. The caterers had washed up after the meal but there were glasses everywhere.

Dad yawned, 'I think we should pile everything into the kitchen so the club room looks tidy and come back tomorrow.'

'I thought you were going to pack for your cruise tomorrow,' said Izzy pulling paper cloths off the tables and stuffing them into a refuse sack. She turned over a table, with Dad's help, to put the legs down and then, as they carried it to the store room he said, 'We'll still have plenty of time. Your Mum's got neat piles of clothes everywhere, all ready to put in the cases'

'It's going to feel really flat after this brilliant evening and then you and Mum going away for three weeks.'

'We did ask you if you wanted to come but you refused.'

'I know and I don't really want to trail around after you when I'm quite capable of staying at home on my own. Anyway cruising is for old, rich people.' She grinned and waited for the explosion but Dad grinned back. 'It's nearly one o'clock and I really can't be bothered to rise to that, Izzy. This all looks fine let's lock up and go home. I could sleep for a week.'

Sunday morning the alarm went early and Jason cursed as he struggled to turn it off. 'Uncivilised, seven thirty on a Sunday.'

'Just one more day and we can be decadently civilised on holiday. I'll make some tea and then we must make a move. The Club House has to be tidy before everyone comes to race.'

Catherine shrugged into a light wrap and went downstairs. Jason lay listening to her emptying the dishwasher and the hum of the kettle. She arrived back with a mug of tea and a little medicine cup of pills. 'There you go and don't forget to take your pills.'

'Thanks, love, did you take some tea to Izzy?'

'No I thought we could handle the clearing up and let her sleep.'

'OK, I'll drink this and then get up'.

Catherine nodded and went downstairs to drink her tea to the quiet of her I-pad. She liked to start the day with Face Book and was not disappointed. Several people had posted pictures of the party, happy faces obviously enjoying themselves. Her peace was interrupted by a bleary eyed daughter. 'Why didn't you wake me? Is there any water left in the kettle?'

'We thought you'd like to sleep in while Dad and I cleared up.'

'Well that was a kind thought but I heard him going into the bathroom and I'm happy to help. Shall I make some toast?'

Dad arrived in the kitchen just as the second round of toast popped up so he sat at the table and helped himself to butter and marmalade. 'So are you going in for any races today, Izzy?'

'I'd like to but I didn't know if I should, seeing as it's your last day before the holiday.'

'That's not a problem as long as you can get a crew.'

'Cool, I'll text Mark. He's painfully shy but really knows how to sail.'

'I think he's sweet on you,' said Mum.

'That's such an old fashioned phrase Mum and he's still a kid. Anyway I'll go and get my gear together.'

They managed to wash the glasses and clean all the surfaces before the organisers for the race day arrived. There was a catering rota and the Sunday team provided snacks, drinks and lunches. When the couple on duty arrived they were pleased to see everything tidy. They chatted together and Izzy helped because she was staying for the day but Mum and Dad excused themselves and drove home to pack.

Whilst waiting for Phil, Jenny and Mark she bought a coffee and wandered around the clubroom remembering how magical it had been just the night before. She stood in front of cabinets holding sailing trophies and various nautical artefacts and noticed that the brass ones were heavily tarnished and decided to offer to clean them.

'Hi Izzy, where's your Dad?' Izzy smiled at Uncle Phil and told him they were packing.

'Yes, I'd forgotten, they're sailing with more luxury than usual. Well Mark's rigging our boat, have you done yours?'

'No I'll go and make a start. She went out and helped Mark pull the yacht to the slipway. When it was safely in the water and moored they went to her Dad's boat, a National 12, the same as Phil's and rigged that.

The first race was going to begin soon so they tossed for who would helm. Mark won and they set off cruising not far from the start line, waiting. They waved to Phil and Jenny but then they concentrated on jostling for position to cross the line first. The wind was about force five so the pace was exciting enough and their delight was enhanced by the appearance of the sun, suddenly hot above them. The water sparkled and the trees lining the banks looked a vivid green.

'This is great. I bet Dad wishes he was out here today. Can we get any more speed, Mark?' They seemed to leap over the water, laughing as it splashed them and finished the race in first place. The rest of the day was just as good and Izzy praised Mark until even his ears became crimson. They hauled the boats out of the water, put everything away and then Phil offered to run Izzy home.

'That would be lovely, thanks. I was just going to text Dad and ask him to pick me up. Are you ready to go now?'

'Just give us five minutes because I want a quick word with Frank. Frank was the commodore and the mention of him reminded Izzy she needed to ask him about the artefacts. They went together and, when Phil had finished, Izzy requested permission and when that was granted asked who had the key. It seemed her Dad kept it so she would have to ask him.

When she got home she forgot about the key as she told them how she and Mark had trounced all the veterans.

'Well done Izzy. Will you keep going while we're away?'

'Course I will. They'll all be baying for our blood next week and we must try to keep our position.'

'I can remember when Phil and I were the top youngsters but then we got older and heavier. Finally we stopped sailing together, mainly because Jenny learned to sail and was much lighter than me.'

'Changing the subject,' said Mum. 'Dinner is ready and we will all have to have an early night because we need to get up at a silly hour to get to the airport.'

'So what time, exactly, do we need to leave?' asked Izzy.

'Five forty-five should give us enough time because we need to be there by six thirty. I'm pleased you're driving us because I always get anxious waiting for taxies.'

'It's a no-brainer. If I take you I get to use the car while you're away. That's worth getting up early for.'

The following morning they went without breakfast, loaded the car with two large cases and Izzy drove them to the airport. They unloaded quickly and checked that Izzy had a debit card to get out of the drop-off car park. Dad solemnly handed her some pound coins to cover the cost then there was a flurry of hugs and they dragged their cases to the terminal door.

Izzy felt a twinge of loneliness as she turned to get back into the car but it waned when she started the engine and drove to the barrier. She used her card, the barrier lifted and as she accelerated she revelled in her freedom.

When she arrived home her stomach was demanding food so she garaged the car and went into the kitchen. It felt quiet so she put the radio on as she scrambled some eggs and took her breakfast into the living room.

Breakfast was never normally so relaxed, she thought, and enjoyed it to the accompaniment of breakfast television.

Chapter 20

The flight and transfer at Barcelona had gone well and Jason and Catherine embarked, found their cabin and lay on the bed, grinning.

'No wonder Sonia goes on about cruising all the time. So far this is great.'

'We've yet to find a bar or our restaurant so there's lots to discover. When we've unpacked we can explore. Let's look at that welcome letter.' Jason read aloud,

'There will be an emergency drill at 4pm, please look on your door for your muster station and make your way there with your life jackets.

The dress code tonight is informal. There will be a welcome show in the theatre at 8pm and 10pm with your host, Max, and The Lollypops, our own singers and dancers.'

Jason turned his head towards Catherine. 'Seems a little like a holiday camp. I expect any minute a tannoy to announce something and the disembodied voice shout, 'Hi de hi'.' Just as he spoke there was an announcement telling everyone that the ship was about to sail. They laughed so much they missed most of it.

'I think he said we're about to sail. Let's go on deck and watch them casting off,' said Jason.

They left the cabin and went down the stairs to the promenade deck and joined others lounging against the rail. There was music playing and a waiter was moving deftly amongst the people offering glasses of champagne. Jason fetched two glasses and brought them back to Catherine. 'It's really easy to spend money. You just give him your key card and sign a chit.'

Suddenly the ship gave a long, deafening blast on its horn, making everyone jump and then laugh. There was no sensation of movement but the gap between the ship's side and the quay slowly widened. They were on their way.

Izzy had an early lunch and then went to work. She was on the afternoon shift from two until ten, loading shelves in Asda. Holiday jobs were not easy to get and she was both grateful and determined to do well, in the hope they would employ her again. This was her second week and she had begun to enjoy herself. The manager, Harry, seemed friendly and everyone liked and respected him.

'You'll get on fine,' he said at her interview, 'if you work hard and don't chat except at break times.'

At first she thought it meant everything had to be done in silence and she was frightened to speak so the other workers got the impression she was stuck up but Rachel, who often worked near her, put her right. On one of her breaks she sat with her and explained,

'We can talk as much as we like now, on our breaks. When we're working the odd remark here and there, as you're going back to collect more stock is fine.'

'Thanks for telling me that. It'll make things easier.'

'So do you have any hobbies? I do Zumba and Yoga.'

'That's very energetic. You must be fit, Rachel. I go sailing most weekends and like to walk when we go on holiday.'

'I've never tried sailing and don't see how you can unless you own a boat. Do you have your own boat?'

'No it's my dad's. He's been sailing forever and eventually Mum got involved but not until I was older. She went on the same course as me when I was ten and we both saw why Dad was so keen. It isn't just sailing about the lake it's the racing that gets to you. Last Sunday Mark and I won all our races and felt brilliant.'

'Wow you must be good. So is this Mark your boyfriend?'

'No he's just a kid. I haven't got a boyfriend at the moment. What about you?

'Me?' Rachel laughed loudly causing others in the canteen to look around and smile. I've been married three years and have a two year old.'

'Oh, I thought you were about my age.'

'Probably am, nineteen. What about you?'

'I had my eighteenth on Saturday but I've only just left school. You've been very busy.'

'Yes, well I got pregnant at sixteen but I was lucky 'cause Terry really loved me, and now we're doing all right.' She stood up. 'Anyway times up let's get back to work.'

Izzy looked forward to more chats during breaks times but thought about Rachel's life and vowed to finish her education before getting involved with anyone. Just two months and she could take her place at Lancaster University, if her grades were good enough.

That evening, at the end of her shift, Izzy was glad to go home and make herself a cup of tea. The house seemed uncomfortably quiet so she put the television on and sat in Mum's favourite chair to watch it. She flicked through the channels but there was nothing to hold her attention and her thoughts returned to her party. She remembered her intention to clean the artefacts and trophies. If Dad had a key to the cabinet had he also got a key to the clubhouse? She turned the television off and went into his study. The keys were together, labelled, in the desk drawer. As she turned off the lights, checked the doors and went up to bed, Izzy decided to go to the sailing club the following morning.

The next day the sun shone and it felt really hot as Izzy pocketed the keys and carried a sturdy plastic box to the car. The journey was only twenty minutes and as she parked it was obvious that she was alone. Inside the clubhouse she unlocked the cabinets and lifted each item carefully. She wished she had brought some bubble wrap to keep them from jostling and getting scratched. In the kitchen Izzy found paper and a pen and wrote a note explaining what she was doing so it was clear they had not been burgled. The box was heavy as she put it into the boot of the car and she drove home carefully so the trophies didn't tumble about.

There was still an hour before she needed to have lunch so she made herself a cup of coffee and searched the kitchen cupboards for brass and sliver cleaner. She found both but the brass cleaner was almost empty so she would need to buy some at work that afternoon.

Armed with clean rags she began with the telescope and worked hard getting it to gleam and was very pleased with the difference she

121

had made. She wrapped it in some newspaper, put it back in the box and began to clean the sand timer. It was tricky with the brass pillars and she was only part way through cleaning it when it was time for lunch. It could be left until later she realised and washed her hands.

That evening when she came home she thought about finishing the timer but was feeling tired so she went to bed. There was no urgency; she had all the rest of the week to finish cleaning them.

India 1857

The curtains were closed against the sun and there was a stationary fan in the centre of the ceiling. It felt airless and stuffy to Izzy as she looked at the scene. There were two people arguing, a young woman sitting with embroidery on her knee, dressed in Victorian clothes and an army officer standing, looking down at her. The room was over furnished with chairs, cushions and a chaise longue. There were several occasional tables and an oppressive, dark oak sideboard. A mottled mirror on the wall behind the officer failed to relieve the general dinginess.

'I'm not leaving you Cecil. Other army wives have babies as they travel with the regiment and I'm going to do just that.'

'Darling, you're not any other army wife. You're my wife and I love you and our baby to be. Please be sensible.'

'I don't see this situation is any worse than Rangoon so I'm not sailing back to England if that's what you're suggesting.' Jane stood abruptly and moved to the bell to ring for Emily. Cecil stood, stiff with annoyance, unwilling to discuss this further in front of the servant. He watched with a sour face as Emily entered and bobbed a curtsy.

'Ah, Emily,' said Jane. We would like tea and some of that seedy cake if there's any left.'

'There is some left, memsahib and I'll make tea. How may people are taking tea?'

Jane curled her lip and said sharply, 'Two, of course,' then added, as the girl had not moved, 'That's all, you can go.'

She bobbed a small curtsey and left them.

'It will not be for ever, Jane,' continued Cecil. 'This is going to be much worse than Rangoon. It's not just a war, army against army. These natives hate the British. They've been killing women and children. Major Shankin is despatching his wife on Wednesday and I have arranged that you go with her. You can both sail on your father's ship, 'Daphne', from Calcutta and you'll have an armed escort all the way.'

At that moment Emily arrived with the tea and cake so Jane bit back her anger, for the moment. As soon as they were alone in the room again she hissed her disgust. 'So I have no choice. You've arranged it all and I must just be a good little wife and accept it.' She stood as she said this and went to the door. Cecil winced as she shouted, 'If you want me I'll be in my room, packing,' and she slammed the door behind her.

Izzy woke up and wondered at her ability to conjure such an unusual and vivid dream. Why would she dream about people in India? She thought about television programmes, books and articles in magazines but couldn't remember anything that could have triggered it. The bedside clock said it was only 2.15 but she felt so wide-awake she got up and went downstairs. In the kitchen she winced at the brightness of the light and quickly microwaved a mug of milk, which was guaranteed to help her go back to sleep. She walked about, blowing the milk that was too hot and then went into Dad's study, picked up her I-Pad and searched for, 'uprisings in India in Victorian times'.

There had been problems and riots in Rangoon, Burma and the 84th Regiment of foot, had been marched from there all the way to India and eventually arrived at Lucknow. There were some grisly details of women and children being murdered and she decided this was the stuff of nightmares, read no more and went back to bed.

The following morning Izzy woke later than usual, missed breakfast and made a cooked brunch of fried egg, bacon, toast and baked beans. She finished it with a jam tart and then felt guilty at having eaten so much. Perhaps she should take up running like Dad.

Sailing was energetic and tiring but that was just once a week. The only thing she could do to make up for it was to walk to work, briskly.

When she arrived she was really hot and happily agreed to the request to work in the cold store. They gave her thick gloves and a coat and after an hour she began to long for a chance to go out into the sunshine. But, she had vowed to be amenable and work hard so she was as cheerful as she could be when her face was so cold it was hard to move her lips into a smile.

That evening it was still not fully dark when she walked home and she broke into a jog. She challenged herself to keep going until she got to the station. It was up hill and she struggled but almost got there before she had to slow to a walk.

'Hi, Isabelle.'

She looked up, saw Andrew from school and stopped with a smile. 'Wow, Andy! I haven't seen you for at least a year. What've you been doing?'

'Do you fancy a drink? There's still time before last orders.'

'Yes, that'd be great, we've got some catching up to do.'

They crossed the road and went into a wine bar. It was not very busy so they had a choice of tables. A waitress came up for their order and Izzy chose a white wine, Andrew a lager. When she had gone they both began to talk at once and laughed.

'You first,' said Izzy. 'I've missed seeing you at school. Are you at Uni somewhere?'

'I'm sorry I left without telling you what I was doing but we could leave immediately our A levels were finished and I was so keen to start my new life I didn't think about saying goodbye. Anyway I wasn't going far away if I got my grades.'

'Did you get them?'

'Yes, two A stars and an A.'

'Wow, I knew you were clever but that's fantastic. I won't do anywhere near as well as that. Surely you could've gone to Oxford or Cambridge with those grades.'

'Maybe but I'd made up my mind to go to Lancaster, just a few hours drive from home. You see my Dad's got cancer and I didn't want to be too far away in case Mum needed me.'

Izzy's smile dropped to a look of sympathy. 'I'm really sorry Andy.' She reached her hand across the table and held his. How's he doing now?'

'Good at the moment; he had months of treatment but now he's in remission, thank God.'

'I'm pleased for you,' she said as she took her hand back. 'What are you studying then?'

'It's all sciences. I'm keen on doing medical research and, funnily enough, I wanted to do that before I knew about Dad.' Izzy nodded imaging him in a vivisection laboratory and shuddered inwardly, hoping that wouldn't be the case.

'Your turn now; you've finished school and working or waiting to go to Uni?'

'Both, I've just finished the late shift at Asda and am hoping to go to, wait for it, Lancaster.'

'That's great we'll be able to meet there. I'd like that,' he said with genuine pleasure. 'I can't believe I didn't ask you out when we were at school but there's still time, unless you've already got a boyfriend.'

'No I haven't.' She thought of her conversation with Rachel and grinned.

'Is that a yes then?'

'I'd like to go out with you but it's not very easy because I work from two until ten six days a week. I only get Sundays off and usually go sailing then.'

'In that case we can start by having a coffee somewhere in a morning. When would be good?'

'I'm not busy tomorrow. Shall we make it 10.30? Have you got a favourite café?'

'What about meeting at the entrance to M and S and then we can choose where to go.' He got his phone out of his pocket. 'Let's swap numbers.' When that was done they stood up to go and Andy offered to walk her home.

'There's no need I don't live far away but thanks for offering.' She was about to move away when he caught her arm, pulled her towards him and kissed her. Her body reacted wantonly; she kissed him back and then felt a wave of panic. It was all happening too fast.

Finally they parted and when she got home she went straight to bed and her dreams were of Andy.

They were making love and his body was slim, a beautiful brown with dark body hair. He probably had some Asian genes she thought but then that sense of panic came over her and she woke up. With dreams like that I'd better get myself some protection but I think the pill takes a month to work before you're safe. I'll book an appointment at the clinic before seeing Andy for coffee. That decision helped her to feel in control of herself and she slept until her alarm woke her at nine.

She rang the clinic whilst the kettle boiled and a nurse could see her the following day. Now what should she wear for her date? At first she chose cream, linen trousers to wear, wanting to look attractive for Andy, changed her mind and swapped them for darker ones. There may not be time to change before going to work she thought. Rachel will be surprised enough when she sees me with make up on. I think I'll tell her about Andy.

The coffee date was a success and they agreed to meet again on Saturday night at the same wine bar. Doing her washing and then visiting the clinic filled Friday morning and on Saturday morning she looked again at the pile of artefacts and trophies left to clean. Somehow the task seemed larger than it did; her enthusiasm had waned.

They could all be returned tomorrow when she went sailing so it would be worth the effort. She pulled on rubber gloves, finished the sand timer and began to work on the silver cups. They were standing all over the table when the house phone went.

'Hi Izzy it's Phil. I'm afraid Mark's got some awful stomach bug and will not be up to sailing tomorrow. We won't be going either, obviously, so perhaps you can crew for someone else.'

'Don't worry Uncle Phil I can do that or even miss it for a week.'

'How are you managing without your Mum and Dad? Holding wild parties every night?'

'I wish! No I'm fine. I've been meeting a friend from school and, don't tell them, but I'm quite enjoying having the house to myself.'

'I won't breathe a word. Ok, better go, see you next week then, bye.'

Normally no sailing would have made her feel wretched but she was delighted to have a whole day free to be with Andy. She sent him a text, made herself a coffee and sat at the kitchen table looking balefully at the smeary trophies waiting to be polished. There was no real hurry now she wasn't going to the club tomorrow. Then she gave herself a telling off donned her gloves again and began to rub each one until it gleamed.

Her phone pinged and she read he was free on Sunday and would she like a walk in the Dales and lunch in a country pub. Texting in rubber gloves was not possible so she replied quickly and then put them back on and finished the trophies. She decided she needed another box so she could separate the artefacts that came from one glass case and the trophies that were from a larger one. That would make both boxes lighter and it would be easier when she came to put them back.

At work, later that day, Izzy acquired a stout cardboard box and could hardly wait to tell Rachel about Andy.

'He sounds lovely, clever too. You should keep hold of him 'cos he'll get a good job.'

'Well it's a bit early to think of the future. I need to get to know him a bit better and I'm hoping to go to Uni myself in October. I really like him, though.'

'I remember feeling all moony over my Terry; couldn't think of anything else. Me Mum was so cross with me, kept telling me to wake up and asking me what planet I was on.' She laughed and Izzy joined her. Break times were fun when she was with Rachel.

At the end of her shift she jogged to the wine bar and found Andy waiting for her. He offered her a drink but she insisted on buying them. 'I'm earning and you don't seem to be. I thought everyone at Uni got summer jobs.'

'I did try. I got two weeks labouring on a building site and I hated it. The work was really hard and my blisters were agony. There's not much to see for it now.' He held out his hands and she could see the marks even though the lighting was subdued. 'But the pay was worth it and if they get short handed I'm top of the list.'

'Well stacking shelves doesn't pay that well but it's for six weeks and I'm trying to be careful with money to help if I get my grades.'

'What subjects did you go for?'

'Geography, English and History and my aim is either teaching or librarian. I can keep my options open for now because if I go for teaching I can do another year.'

Andy nodded. 'I remember your dad at school taking me for PE. I think he liked me because I was a speedy runner and usually did well on sports days, but I was never any good on the football field. What was it like going to the same school as your dad?'

'It didn't bother me because he did mostly boys games and us girls had Jenny.'

'Who was Jenny? I was never on first name terms with any teachers.'

'She married my dad's best friend, Phil. I've known them both all my life. You would know her as Mrs Dunstan. She taught music as well as PE.'

'Yes, well that explains why you were always teacher's pet.'

'I wasn't.' She laughed and pretended to take a swipe at him. 'Anyway, changing the subject, let's arrange tomorrow. Would you like me to drive?'

'Do you have your own car?'

'No but I can use Dad's.'

'What just like that without asking?'

'I can use it as much as I like during the next fortnight because he and Mum are on holiday.'

'Are they now. So let's go back to your place.' He was grinning, wolfishly and she shook her head.

'I don't think so but I'll pick you up at 10 tomorrow.'

When she got home Izzy was cross with herself for revealing her parents were away. Then again how long was she going to stay a virgin? Most of her school friends said they'd done it and sneered at her lack of experience. Perhaps this was the right time, with Andy.

She went to bed and tried to imagine being with him in her Mum and Dad's room. No she couldn't do that. The spare bedroom had a double bed and that would be better. It was a while before she fell asleep and then she half woke to throw off the covers. It was unbearably hot.

Chapter 21

India 1857

The road glared white and shimmered as Izzy stood looking into the distance. Something was approaching slowly but she couldn't see what it was, dazzled by the sun.

The image became clearer, soldiers on horseback and two carts. There were also two women, riding side-saddle, with long flowing dresses and holding parasols. When they came closer she stepped off the road onto the scrubby grass but they slowed as a woman called out for the entourage to stop. They were all looking at her and she squirmed under their scrutiny. Finally one of the ladies spoke to her.

'What on earth are you doing out here in the middle of nowhere dressed in nothing but your shift?'

'I don't know,' Izzy replied.

'Perhaps you've had a too much sun. Anyway you're obviously British and we can't leave you to be manhandled by, erm, well never mind. You'd better get up on the cart next to Emily and we'll talk as we ride if you're up to it.'

Izzy climbed up onto the cart she had pointed to and Emily shifted over to make space. Before taking up the reigns again she reached back into the cart for a straw hat and a wrap. Izzy put them on, glad to have something to protect herself from the searing heat. They moved on and the woman who had spoken to her waited for the cart to reach her before moving and then she kept pace. 'My name is Jane Carstairs and my travelling companion is Mrs Amelia Shankin. Can you remember your name?'

'Yes, I'm Isabelle Brownlow and thank you for rescuing me. Where are you heading?'

'We are on our way to Calcutta to take a ship to England. You are welcome to accompany us if that suits you. Perhaps when you regain your memory you may change your mind but a white woman alone is in great danger. Our husbands are both army officers, which is why we have this escort.'

She spurred her horse and moved away obviously not wanting to talk to her any longer.

Izzy had recognised her as the woman arguing with her husband in the stuffy room. What was happening? If this was a dream it was very real. She could smell the horses and Emily's sweat, or was it her own?

There was silence for a while apart from the clatter of horses' hooves and the creaking of the carts and then Emily said, 'I saw you in the drawing room a few days ago. Memsahib did not include you in the tea and I thought that was odd.'

'Well, if you saw me why didn't you say something then?'

'It was not my place to ask about visitors. We've been travelling many days. I do not see how you can be on the road with no horse.'

Izzy sighed. 'I don't know how I got on the road. I must have lost my memory as Jane, I mean Mrs Carstairs, said.'

They were approaching the town and the travellers halted while two soldiers at the front went ahead to check that all was well and if there was some accommodation to be had. Emily got down and took some water to the two ladies and then offered Izzy some. It was warm, tasted earthy but was very welcome. In the lull Izzy noticed her feet felt itchy. She held them out in front of her and saw they were red and blotchy. She tucked them as far behind her as she could to put them in the shade.

It was a long, silent wait in the relentless sun but there was no other option. Eventually they saw the soldiers returning and, as all seemed to be safe, they rode on into the town of Allahabad. They were going to stay in an English Hotel and hoped to get there before the light faded.

'Once it gets dark,' said Emily, 'it becomes very dangerous. The people are not happy with the British ruling them and our soldiers are very angry about the ammunition they are expected to use.'

Izzy realised she was going to explain more but Jane rode up and said, 'You must stop gossiping, Emily. Miss Brownlow is not to be treated as an equal.'

Emily's chin dropped down onto her chest. Was she embarrassed or angry? Izzy couldn't tell but she was full of indignation and her tone was sharp as she said, 'Emily was trying to explain to me why the night was even more dangerous than daylight. It was not gossip.'

'It is not your place to either talk to my servant or to argue with me young lady. Do not forget you are with us because we felt anxious on your behalf.'

Izzy's chin came up defiantly but she said nothing, realising the truth of Jane's words.

They arrived at the hotel and the soldiers helped the ladies dismount and one came up to Izzy and held her hand as she alighted from the cart. The carts were emptied and various people from the hotel took the luggage as the ladies went into the cool of the lobby. Jane seemed to be the leader because she spoke to the receptionist and asked for three rooms plus servant accommodation. As it was being arranged Izzy looked at the Victorian splendour and hoped there was some kind of bathroom she could use.

The need to go to the bathroom was urgent and Izzy woke. She tried to turn over but was tangled in the sheet. There was no sheet just a light duvet. She sat up, in her room at home and unwound the wrap Emily had given her. Now fully awake she put on the light and went to the bathroom. When she sat on the toilet she saw her feet were red and they began to itch.

She felt bewildered and scared. Dreams could be vivid, even frightening but they finished when you woke up. How could she have a shawl and sunburnt feet from a dream?

She went downstairs and made a cup of tea. They had travelled for hours with just a drink of water and she was starving. As she put bread in the toaster Izzy was aware of the bizarreness of her thoughts but decided to concentrate on her physical needs. She was going to choose marmalade but thick chocolate spread with its rich sweetness seemed preferable.

Some of the laden toast was already eaten before she reached the lounge and curled up in Mum's chair. Would Mum be able to explain what had happened if she was here? Somehow she doubted that any one could.

It was light outside and very early in the morning but returning to bed was not an option. She picked up her phone and saw she had two texts. Andy just said he was looking forward to their walk. They had made their arrangements the night before but she was glad he'd thought of her before going to sleep. The other one had been sent just a few minutes ago and was from aunty Sonia. Obviously she was an early riser or just couldn't sleep. She read it.

Hi Izzy, Mum asked me to check if you were OK. Can I come over for a coffee on Monday morning? X

Izzy realised how much she was now missing her parents and wrote back quickly saying she would love to see her. She then texted Mum asking if they were having fun and assuring them that she was fine.

Now she felt the need for a shower to wash away the grime of her journey and her nightdress needed to go in the dirty washing.

An hour later she had stripped her bed, having found it gritty with dusty sand and the washing machine was whirring round. The bed was made up with fresh sheets and the shawl carefully folded at the foot of it. She hoped that a good long walk with Andy would help her to forget, at least for a while.

Downstairs she took her hiking boots from the cupboard and got everything ready for the walk including her anorak. It was a dull day, which would be a relief after the heat of last night. It might even be chilly, she thought. She was picking Andy up and had not told him their destination. He was going on a mystery tour. They had laughed at the idea and he said he didn't care where they went.

When they arrived at How Stean Gorge he was delighted, saying he'd not been there for years. He remembered, as a boy, being scared to go through the cave because it was dark. But they were not exploring the gorge itself today. They had a coffee in the café and then began the walk. Izzy set off really quickly and Andy struggled to keep up.

'Have you got a train to catch or an appointment to keep? I'm almost running. Are you all right?'

'No, not really, I had a horrible dream that's really upset me and somehow I feel I must exercise hard to forget it. Can you just let me do it and, hopefully, I'll feel better.'

'Ok but wait for me now and again so I haven't done the entire walk on my own.'

She kissed him quickly and then slowly.

'Perhaps I can help you relax and you won't need this route march.'

'Maybe later but for now I'm moving on.'

He followed her up the hill and found he was not as fit as he thought, his breathing was laboured and he needed to stop half way. She waited for him at the top and they walked along the ridge together.

'Do you want to tell me about your dream? Perhaps it would help.' She shook her head and that seemed to stop all conversation. Eventually she managed to stay in the present and said she hadn't planned anywhere to have lunch.

'There's a couple of cafés and some pubs in Pately Bridge if you'd like a proper Sunday roast,' he said.

'That sounds good. I've missed Mum's cooking this week. Mmm I can almost smell roast beef already. Come on it's downhill all the way now.' That wasn't quite true but Andy kept with her and held her hand. She found that comforting and almost told him what had happened that night but he was a scientist, not a dreamer and she felt sure he would laugh at her.

The pub meal was delicious and Izzy got her roast beef with all the trimmings and luscious dark gravy. Andy wanted to share a bottle of wine but she reminded him she was the driver so she had cola whilst he had a pint of Yorkshire brewed ale. They shared the cost and she invited him to come to her house and have a coffee or tea. He agreed readily saying he would walk home afterwards to save her using the car again.

As soon as they shut the front door Andy put his arms around her. 'I want to make love to you so much I am almost bursting. Please tell me if you feel the same?'

'I do but I'm also a bit scared.'

'Why, I would never hurt you. Are you afraid of me?'

'No you make me feel safe but I'm still a virgin.'

He kissed her gently. 'You know I'm not very experienced so we could learn together. Have you any wine? It would be good to have the glass we wanted earlier and we don't have to rush.'

She pulled away from him, led him into the dining room and opened a cupboard full of red wine and spirits. 'What would you suggest for relaxation?' she asked smiling.

'Have you any Rioja? Let me see. No but there's gin and a bottle of tonic. Do you like that? '

'Yes but I'm not drinking on my own am I? You must have one too.' She collected glasses, gin and tonic and mixed the drinks in the kitchen adding ice.'

While she was doing that he looked in the boxes and unwrapped the timer. This is a beautiful piece of work.'

'Please don't put any fingerprints on that I've spent ages polishing it. All these things belong to the sailing club and I must take them back soon. They were so tarnished I decided to bring them home for some TLC.' She handed him a drink, took the timer from him and wrapped it again.

They went into her lounge with their drinks and she put on some music. The effect of the alcohol began to make both of them relaxed and Andy slipped his hand under her T-shirt and tried to undo her bra. She giggled and did it for him.

'I just need more practice he whispered and then his hands explored her soft breasts and she became aroused. She took off her top and he removed his. The feeling of skin against skin was lovely and Izzy felt it was right; he was right. She was ready to go further and pulled away from him and wriggled out of all the rest of her clothes. He gazed at her with admiration. 'You are so beautiful. Are you happy to do this here or do you want to go to bed?'

'This is fine, the rug's soft and I'm not cold.' They kissed and kissed then he sucked her breast and made her gasp. She pressed her body against his and then everything happened so quickly she nearly forgot. 'Stop, please just for a moment we need a condom.'

'Don't worry I have one here.' He fiddled putting it on then he entered her and it hurt but then she arched her back and let herself savour all the new sensations. When it was over they stayed in each other's arms, silent for a long time then he whispered, 'So now you know what sex is all about. What did you think of it?'

She smiled, lazily. 'It was unexpectedly lovely. I always thought the mechanics of it seemed almost unpleasant but I hadn't understood the excitement and the need you feel to be satisfied.'

'So you wouldn't mind doing it again sometime?'

He began to caress her again and she moved away. 'Yes but not now, I'm starving; our Sunday dinner seems ages ago. It was ages ago it's eight o'clock. Shall I make us some sandwiches?'

He nodded and she grabbed her clothes and ran upstairs to the bathroom. She washed and put on her nightdress and light dressing gown then went into the kitchen. When she came back into the lounge with the food and two cups of tea Andy was dressed and they sat happily eating and enjoying the special closeness they felt.

Soon after they had eaten he went home and Izzy went to bed. She looked balefully at the Indian wrap, moved it to her dressing table and snuggled down under the covers thinking of Andy.

Chapter 22

Izzy struggled to open her eyes as she heard someone was knocking. The bedroom door opened and in walked Emily. 'The Memsahib asks you to hurry and get dressed. I bring you clothes and shoes. Please hurry.'

Izzy felt slightly sick when she stood up and looked around her at the small room. There was a washstand with a bowl and some water, like something from a museum but there was no time she must hurry. The cold water made her feel better. She picked up the underwear; a kind of bodice thing and long pants. She sighed and pulled them on. There were several petticoats and a grubby looking cream muslin dress that fitted quite well but was too long. The tiny mirror on the washstand showed her looking like a middle class Victorian woman, apart from her hair, which was an unkempt mess. There was no brush so she would just have to do.

When she entered the dining room Jane was pacing up and down and stopped when she saw her. 'Please drink some tea, eat something as quick as you can because we have had news of a raiding party heading this way. They'll kill us. This is what my husband was trying to protect me from. All the miles we've travelled and we're still in danger. I feel like turning round and going back. I don't know what to do for the best.'

'We have the protection of the soldiers, don't we?'

'Yes but most of them are Indian and cannot be trusted not to turn rebel on us.'

Izzy frowned. 'I don't really understand why soldiers in British uniforms would want to turn against us.'

'I will tell you more later but now we must go. Mrs Shankin is outside already waiting for us.'

Once again Izzy jolted along on the cart with Emily who kept biting her lip and looking behind and all around. Her fear was catching and Izzy felt anxious too. They were approaching a tiny hamlet with chickens pecking for whatever they could find in the dry earth and dirty children squatting, their big brown eyes watching, as they came near. Izzy could smell a wood fire and saw the smoke drifting up in the hot, still air. It was so quiet. The dust muffled the horses' hooves so the crack of a rifle was shockingly loud. There was a shout of pain and one of the soldiers fell forwards in his saddle. His body flopped to one side, his feet were jammed in the stirrups and prevented him from falling off.

There was confusion as women grabbed the children, the chickens squawked and flapped while Mrs Shankin wailed hysterically. It was an ambush and they were sitting targets. The soldiers loaded their rifles. Izzy jumped off the cart and ran round to Emily's side. 'Get down and hide with me.' She shouted, 'Jane, come to us or the...' She stopped speaking as the next shot silenced Mrs Shankin who tottered and fell to the ground.

Jane scrambled off her horse, hesitated as she saw her companion's head pooled in blood, then ran, bending low, to where Izzy and Emily hid. In the exchange of fire Izzy looked around for a better place to hide. If the horses bolted they would be exposed. A very old man in a dhoti caught her eye and nodded his head. She grabbed Jane's hand. 'It'll be safer over there. Let's run when they start firing again.'

At the first explosion they ran into the dark doorway and the old man showed them another door at the back. 'Many places to hide out there, may your God protect you.' They ran through and Izzy headed down hill where she could see some wilting trees. They slithered into a dusty ditch gasping from running and fear.

The light was fading and it had been quiet for hours but they dare not move.

'When it's fully dark I think it'll be safe to go but without horses we cannot travel all the way to Calcutta. I don't know what to do for the best. Why have none of our soldiers looked for us?' Jane's whispering voice had lifted almost to a squeak and Izzy realised she was crying. She put an arm around her. 'Perhaps Emily could slip into the village and find out what's happening. The man that helped us might do so again.'

'Yes, that's sensible. We are too obvious with our white skin but Emily could go unnoticed. Will you do that for us?' She looked at her servant who nodded and stood carefully peering around. There was no sign of life so she climbed out of the ditch and went back up the hill.

The moon was high and bright and they clearly saw her return with the old man a few minutes later. He was carrying a water bottle. They stood up but he gestured for them to stay there and he crouched with them in the ditch.

'Your soldiers are all dead as well as white memsahib. The rebels took the horses but left the carts, after searching them. They seemed in a hurry to get away from the village. They headed south, leaving us to bury your dead.'

'Did they take the horses hitched to the carts?' asked Jane. He shook his head and gestured them to follow him back to the road. The horse's heads were down. They needed rest, food and water before they could go any further but when she asked he said, 'No I cannot help you any more. You must leave now. It is not safe for us, or you, if you stay. Five miles on there will be water and grazing for horses. I have food and water for you ladies. Please, go now.'

They whispered their thanks and Jane got onto her cart, Emily took the other and Izzy sat with Jane. The bright moon showed the road clearly and they plodded on until, just as they had been told, they found a spring with water and vegetation. They unhitched the horses and after they had had a drink tied them beside some scrubby grass.

'Now,' said Jane. 'Let's see what he gave us to eat.' She unwrapped the small bundle to reveal chapattis and goat's cheese. They shared it all and refilled their water bottle at the spring. The carts were not long enough for the women to lie out fully in them, but Jane and Izzy curled up and fell into an exhausted sleep while Emily kept watch.

Monday, England

Izzy opened her eyes and noticed the, now familiar, feeling of queasiness. She was not surprised to find herself fully dressed in Victorian costume and wasted no time in removing it and placing it with the shawl. I was lucky Jane didn't notice I'd lost that shawl, she thought. I'm sure it must have cost a lot of money. Her double life felt less strange this time and as she showered she mused on the privations of Victorian plumbing and revelled in the flow of constant hot water she was enjoying.

In the kitchen she decided toast was not sufficient for someone who had come close to being killed and starved most of the previous day so she cooked scrambled egg and bacon. Later, as she cleared her dishes into the dishwasher, Izzy began to think about the present day. It was Monday so she had to work in the afternoon and Aunty Sonia was coming for coffee.

She found a new packet of biscuits and filled the coffee pot ready to switch on then noticed the trophies. She would return them to the sailing club tomorrow; meanwhile they would not live in the kitchen but in the entrance hall so she would not forget to take them. As she was moving the boxes she heard her phone ping and she hoped the text would be from Andy.

Hi gorgeous. Yesterday was wonderful can we meet tonight after work or tomorrow for coffee?

Izzy felt so confused and exhausted she realised she needed to talk to someone about her night travels and she couldn't tell Andy. She needed some space, some time to think, so she wrote back that she couldn't see him until Wednesday morning. But then she regretted it. She did want to see him but at that moment she wanted to see her mum more.

The emotional rollercoaster proved too much and tears dripped down to her chin. 'This won't do Isabelle Brownlow. Sonia is coming and you must do some cleaning.'

When Sonia rang the doorbell Izzy had just put away the vacuum cleaner. She ran to open the door, hardly letting her cross the threshold before she hugged her tightly. When Izzy let her go Sonia looked at her and said, 'Something has happened to you, hasn't it? Let's have that coffee that smells so good and you can tell me all about it.'

They sat at the kitchen table and Sonia felt her own face draining of colour as she listened to the story.

'I know you must think this is the strangest thing you've ever heard but I can show you my clothes. Come and see.'

They went up to the bedroom and Sonia lifted up the dress, the petticoats and the shawl and then sat on the bed, patting the space beside her. 'I believe everything you've told me, my darling girl and it is not the strangest thing I have ever heard.'

'Really? You mean you know of other people that have lived in two places and times?'

'Well the previous person was in the same place but travelled in time. You see, although I am not an authority, there has to be a portal to go back into the past and I think I know what it is. Did you bring a ship's sand timer into the house?'

'Yes it's in a box in the hallway. I'll fetch it.'

'No! Please don't touch it!' She had almost shouted that and modified her voice, 'At least, not at the moment. You see when you touch it the timer becomes active. Later, when you're asleep it takes you back in time. I need to think about what the best thing to do might be. One thing I do know is that it won't let any harm come to you. I also believe it wants you to do something, or perhaps you've done it by saving Jane and Emily.' She stood up. 'Let's go downstairs; I'd love another cup of coffee if there's any left.'

Izzy felt suddenly lighter and so grateful to Sonia for believing her. She hugged her again. 'There's more coffee and thank you so much.'

'I think I could eat one of those ginger biscuits now. In fact I could probably devour the packet, said Sonia.'

They both laughed as Sonia took two and dunked one in her coffee. 'Sorry I know it's disgusting to dunk but soggy gingers are delicious. I want to think about all you've told me, Izzy. You see I'm not sure if the clothes should remain here. The fact that you have them makes me feel the journey is not yet ended. Perhaps you have to ensure that Jane gets on the ship to England. I want to think about this some more and ring you when I have.

In the meantime don't touch the timer and don't take it back to the sailing club. Will that be ok? I must go now but I will ring soon and don't worry about all this.'

Izzy saw Sonia to the door and looked at her watch. She would need to have lunch soon but first she would text Andy to change their arrangements. Sonia had made her feel much better and now she really wanted to see him. As she prepared a healthy salad for lunch she got a message back.

'Excellent! See you after work tonight, same wine bar.'

Chapter 23

Rome 2033

Jason and Catherine threw a few coins into the Trevi Fountain and stood gazing at the statuary dwarfing the courtyard.

'Did you make a wish?' he asked.

'Yes I wished this holiday could go on for ever.'

'Well it won't come true now you've told me,' he said laughing. 'Come on let's find a café and have a drink; I'm parched.' They found a wine bar and sat outside under the shade of an umbrella. They ordered long cold drinks and when Catherine went inside to find a toilet Jason felt his phone vibrate. The text was from Sonia.

Jason I have a problem and need to talk to you. Izzy has the timer at home, cleaned it and has been travelling back in time to India. She has met Jane. Not sure what to do. Please ring, S x

Catherine returned and saw him with his phone. 'Have you had a text from Izzy?'

'No, one from Sonia; she's been to see Izzy and she's fine.' He hated lying to her but, even after all these years, he couldn't bring himself to tell her about his trips into the past.

'Sonia's lovely isn't she. Perhaps next time we book a cruise we should invite them to come with us. Everyone is very friendly here but it would be nice to have someone we knew really well, especially in the evenings. I saw one advertised in the cruise office, a trip across the Atlantic and three days in New York. What do you think?'

'I think you're getting hooked on cruising. That's probably a whole week at sea without getting off. I'd go crazy. This is the best part of cruising, seeing wonderful places. We've only had one day to see the whole of Rome, and I'd like to return to Italy and spend longer here. We rushed around the Colosseum, had a brief bite to eat then decided the queue was too long to bother with the Sistine Chapel and now we're here and need to return to the ship very soon.

Wouldn't it be heaven to be able to take our time, linger at places instead of dashing?'

'You have a point so let's agree to enjoy what we can now and think of our next holiday later.'

They paid for their drinks, returned to the ship and Jason engineered a time to ring Sonia. 'While you're putting your face on I'll go up to the bar, get some cocktails and find us a seat. Do you want cocktail of the day or something else?'

'Yes please, I seem to like all of them so that'll be fine. I'll only be another five minutes anyway.'

'You say she's got Victorian clothes in our house? My God, Sonia, what does it mean? Should we encourage her to go back and make sure Jane gets on that ship? If she does will that solve everything? And what about the child she's carrying? The family tree doesn't mention that. I don't know what to say. Tell her to take it all back to the Sailing Club and not touch it again!'

Sonia could hear the panic in his voice and tried to keep her own voice steady. She reminded him that the family tree had been changed before and poor Nathan had ceased to exist.

'I'm just scared' said Jason. I know you always said no harm would come to any woman but I love Izzy so much. Supposing she couldn't come back. Supposing Jane doesn't get on that ship and Catherine is dead. There'd be no Izzy. It's terrifying. I don't know what to say! Do you think I should tell Catherine the whole story or not worry her? She's coming. I must go. Bye Sonia.'

'What's the matter Jason? Have we had some bad news? Has something happened to Izzy?' He was silent for a moment and she prompted him. 'Jason answer me, please.

He breathed deeply and said, 'I'm going to tell you a secret I have been keeping from you for eighteen years. You will need to take a big swig of that drink before I start. First Izzy is well but it does concern her.'

Catherine sat slowly down looking at his face. She picked up her drink and then put it down again without tasting it. Her face was white behind the freckles as she watched Jason struggling to begin.

They missed their dinnertime but neither noticed as Jason told Catherine of her death and his discovery of the sand timer's powers. He left nothing out but she suddenly interrupted.

144

'You mean Sonia has known all about this too and you've both kept me in the dark. Does Roger know? Who else knows? I can't believe all this. It's just nonsense.' She stood up, too agitated to sit any longer and he could see tears shining in her eyes. He stood too and tried to take her hand but she snatched it away.'

'Please listen a bit longer, Catherine, because I need your help.' She turned to walk away but he added. 'Izzy has the timer and has been going back in time while we've been here.'

She turned and sat back onto the chair. 'You and Sonia have got Izzy involved? I don't understand; why would you do that?'

'I, we, didn't. She decided to clean all the trophies and artefacts and took them home. When she cleaned the timer it all began.'

Jason continued to explain until Catherine knew as much as he did. She picked up her cocktail and drained it. He did the same waiting anxiously for her to speak.

'I think I need another of those, perhaps two.' She pushed the glass towards him and he stood up without a word.

She downed her second drink and then said, 'So, did I get a good send-off? Who came to my funeral? Does anyone recall these things? Did anyone ask how come I was now alive? My God, Jason there are so many questions my mind is spinning.'

He smiled and said gently, 'I think it's the drinks that are making your head spin. Let's go to the self-service restaurant and get something to eat then I'll answer all your questions.'

Catherine stood and picked up her fourth cocktail to take it with her but Jason stopped her. 'Don't, please, we need to think straight without being addled.'

She nodded and followed him through the bar area to the lift. There were not many people in the restaurant so there was no jostling to see what was on offer. There was so much choice of hot food or cold they both found it hard to choose. They needed food but were so full of anxiety they just stood and looked at it all.

'This is silly,' said Jason. Let's go for a curry.' He filled his plate with a lamb curry and rice then added a naan bread. Catherine copied him being unable to think for herself.

They ate without talking and when half her food was eaten Catherine stopped, sighed, put her knife and fork together and said, 'Right, I'm full, not feeling so tipsy and I need my questions answered.' Jason nodded and she began. 'First who knows about all this apart from you and Sonia?'

'No-one but now you know and we will have to tell Izzy.'

'OK, so when you saved me from the accident and you went back all those months did anyone notice?'

'No, just Sonia, and me; we found we could still remember those months after your accident. Sonia was very upset because she'd met Roger on the cruise and their relationship was very close. She had to meet him all over again and was terrified things might change the second time.'

There was a silence as Catherine tried to digest the facts and Jason dared not fill it. He felt relief at having told her and he was grateful that she had taken it so well. But what should they do next?

'Jason do you think we could leave the ship at the next port and go home? What is our next port?'

'Naples. It's a city so it must have an airport. I will go to reception first thing tomorrow and ask. Now I think we should go to bed. I'm exhausted and you must be too.'

In their stateroom they set an alarm to wake them at six o'clock and ordered a room service breakfast for seven. They decided Jason would find out what he had to do to leave the ship and order a taxi to take them to Naples airport. While he was doing that she would pack.

Their plan worked, their cases were collected and taken to the waiting taxi. They hastily checked they had left nothing and disembarked. At the airport they were lucky to find space on a flight to London but it was landing at Stansted Airport, not Heathrow. They bought the tickets and agreed to get a taxi to their car. It was all costing a lot of money but at that moment nothing seemed more important than getting home.

It was four in the afternoon when they arrived in England. Jason sent a text to Sonia while Catherine texted Izzy.

Izzy heard her phone beep but she was working and ignored it. Then she thought it might be Andy and decided to take a comfort break and read it in the ladies. 'Oh no!'

'Is that you Izzy? Is something wrong?' The toilet flushed and Rachel stood and waited after she had washed her hands. Izzy emerged looking serious.

'So what's happened? Has Andy dumped you?'

'No my parents are in England. They decided to come home early.'

'Weren't they on a cruise round the Med or summat? Must be something's upset them.'

'They don't say why but I think I'm going to have to put Andy off tonight and go straight home.' Rachel nodded and they walked out of the ladies and went back to work. Izzy found it hard to concentrate and during her meal break she went outside to ring Sonia.

' *Mum and Dad are coming home tonight. Have you told them about my time travel? Am I in trouble?'*

Sonia confirmed her parents knew and were worried but tried to reassure her she was not in trouble.

Later that evening she hurried home anxiously feeling guilty that she had spoiled their holiday. What sort of reception was she going to get?

Mum and Dad were sitting in the lounge eating sandwiches and drinking wine. They both stood up and hugged her and she found her eyes filling with tears. Dad handed her a tissue and poured her a glass of wine and Mum pushed the sandwiches towards her.

'It seems you've been having some excitement whilst we've been away. I don't know, we leave you for ten days on your own and everything goes wrong.' He was smiling and his voice was kind.

Izzy began to sob. 'I'm so glad you've come home. I was frightened, thought I was going crazy. Really missed you and Mum.'

'Aunty Sonia helped, didn't she?'

'Yes she said she knew someone who'd gone back into the past like me.'

'She didn't tell you who that was?'

'No, I assumed it was a person I wouldn't know.' Dad nodded and decided to give Izzy a potted version of his experiences. He just told her about buying the timer, cleaning it, as she had done but then jumped to Mum's accident.

'So you see, Izzy, that timer enabled you to be born. Now the problem is what does the timer want you to do? Jane seems to be the key and she is on Mum's family tree. We are not sure if she needs help to get on the ship to England or whether she needs to do something different.'

'She doesn't want to go to England, Dad. She's going to have a baby and she wants to go back and be with her husband. It's dangerous out there. Only three of us now travelling in a country that seems to hate English people. I've never been shot at before.'

She paused and noticed Mum was now crying. 'It's ok Mum, Sonia says no harm will come to me.'

Dad stood up and Izzy sensed some kind of decision was coming. 'I think the reason you still have all the clothes is because this isn't finished. Mum and I agree that you should touch the timer again before you go to bed tonight and wear the clothes. Explanations will be tricky if you arrive in your nighty. How do you feel about that?'

'I think you're right and I'm not scared any more, now I know you've done it and you'll be home when I wake up.'

Chapter 24

India

Izzy woke, aching from sleeping on the hard wood of the cart. Emily whispered to her. 'Memsahib sleeps still but I think I can hear rumble noises. Izzy was alert now and nodded. 'Yes I can hear it too. I think something big is coming along the road. I'll wake Jane.' She pushed Jane's shoulder gently; she stirred and opened her eyes.

'Keep quiet Jane we think something is coming and it might be more rebels. Emily, let's hitch the horses to the carts in case we have to move quickly.' They both knew that a rider on horseback could easily catch a cart but some action seemed necessary. Jane took the water bottles to the spring and while she was away from them Izzy asked Emily why she had an English name?

'It is not my real name. My name is Jhoti. The memsahib once had an English servant called Emily and said she would call me that.'

'Have you been with her a long time?'

'Not all that long, just a few months.'

'In that case I'm surprised you were happy to come on a long dangerous journey.' Emily just shrugged and their conversation ended as Jane returned and they were ready to leave.

'I think we should go now. The noise is still there but doesn't seem to be coming from behind us.'

They set off along the road and the noise became more distinct.

'It sounds like an army on the move, not rebels. Perhaps we could ask them for an escort,' said Jane.

They could see them clearly when they reached a crossroad. Officers were on horseback, soldiers marching, women and children on carts. It was impressive and the three women halted their horses and watched. An officer rode up to them and asked where they were going.

'My husband is Captain Cecil Carstairs of the 84th Regiment of Foot and he sent us to Calcutta with an armed escort but we were ambushed and everyone, except us, was killed. We were hoping you might be able to spare some men to protect us.'

'I'm afraid, Mrs Carstairs, that is out of the question. As you can see we are headed west hoping to meet up with the 84th near Lucknow. The town is under siege and we need all our men. It's also impossible for you ladies to travel alone in this countryside so I'm afraid you will have to come with us. When we have sorted out the problems in Lucknow we may be able to oblige you.' He called two men to show the ladies where to filter into the cavalcade and rode away.

'Well it seems I'll meet my husband sooner than I thought and perhaps he'll let me stay with him. After all we did try really hard to get to Calcutta. I'm quite pleased, really.' Jane was smiling and waved happily to other women travelling near them.

She turned to look at Izzy. 'Have you got any memory back yet, Isabelle? It seems strange that you have been with us for several days but you still cannot tell us what happened to you.'

Izzy shook her head. 'I'm sorry but I really have no idea why I was just standing by the road. Perhaps I was in a previous ambush and the horror was too much for my brain.'

'Yes but you were unharmed, undressed and very clean. It is odd is it not?'

Izzy nodded and made an effort to change the subject. 'So will you still be travelling to England?'

'Not if I can help it. By the time we've travelled to Lucknow and put down the uprising I shall be too near to my time to travel. I'm sorry if this change of circumstance upsets your plans.'

'No, that's fine. I didn't really have a plan of my own.' There was a pause in the conversation and Izzy became aware of sounds, the jingling of harness, the creaking of cartwheels. Somewhere a child cried and was soothed. She felt safe surrounded by soldiers, the sun was hot and she began to close her eyes. They went over a lump in the road and she woke in a panic. Sleeping could mean she goes back to her own time. She must stay awake. Talking, she must keep talking for there was nothing else to do although some women were walking beside carts. How they could stop, even for a moment, without causing chaos?

'So can you tell me now why Indian soldiers in the English army are rebelling?'

'Yes, it's complicated but basically it's religion. Goodness knows we have tried to convert them to Christianity. Christians don't have a problem with taking the caps off the cartridges with their teeth.'

'I'm sorry I don't understand. Why do Muslims or Hindus find this difficult?'

'It's the grease on the cartridge. A rumour began that it was a mixture of cow and hog fat. It's not true but the cow is sacred to Hindus and the pig unclean to both so they were angry. There are other reasons for the uprising but the cartridges, if you forgive the pun, seemed to explode the sepoys into action.' She laughed and Izzy smiled but thought the English of that time must have been very arrogant.

There was a stop for toileting and food but they had nothing to eat and were unsure what to do. They sat on the ground in the shade of their cart and looked bleakly at each other. It was not long before a child of about eight years came up to them shyly and offered them a basket of food and a flask of water. She turned to go but Jane stopped her. 'That's so kind of you. What's your name?'

'Mary.' She fidgeted shyly and looked down at her feet.

'Well, Mary, thank you for bringing us some refreshment and please say thank you to your mother.' The little girl bobbed her head, half nod, half curtsey and ran back to her cart.

They travelled on and on in the afternoon heat that was scarcely relieved when the sun started to go down.

'I've no idea where we are or if there will be anywhere to stay tonight. I'd really like to be able to wash and have a soft bed to sleep on. I'm used to camping with the army, of course, and camp beds are much better than this wooden cart.' Jane sat up tall and peered ahead but could see nothing except more carts and the rears of horses.

A short while later they came to a halt. Soldiers rode back to pass the word that they were entering a village and to be quiet and careful. If it seemed safe they would stay there the night.

It was frightening to play out a scene so similar to the ambush and Izzy sat poised to jump off if there should be any trouble. They moved slowly, seeing bodies and body parts strewn around. Dogs and crows moved warily around the carrion unwilling to leave unless forced to. The stench of blood and putrefaction seemed to thicken the air. There was no living soul in the village; men, women children, babies, all hacked to death. Izzy was sick over the side of the cart. The sight was like a scene from a horror film but she knew it was real. An officer rode back and Jane shouted to him. 'Please, tell me, who was responsible for this carnage?'

His face was grim as he replied, 'It seems to be the work of our own army. This uprising has brought out the beast in both sides. I'm sorry you have to see it but where we are going it could be worse. When my men have checked all the houses we will move on and camp away from here.'

A few hours later tents were pitched in the dark and Izzy and Jane were squeezed in with little Mary's family. Emily was left to fend for herself using their cart once again. As she struggled to go to sleep, fully clothed, Izzy prayed that the timer would whisk her away and she vowed never to use it again.

But when morning came she was still there, in India.

'Jason, Jason!'

'What's up?'

'Izzy, she's still there. She hasn't come back,' said Catherine. She was sitting, in her nightdress, on Izzy's bed, tears dripping down her cheeks. 'What can we do?'

'I don't know. It never happened to me. I was late once and Sonia was here, looking for me.'

'What did Sonia do?'

'I don't think she did anything but she had a dream.'

'Oh. Well that sounds really useful, Jason. Our daughter is stuck in the past and we encouraged her to go. How could we have been so stupid? You must be able to do something to get her back. Go and get that timer.'

Jason left the room anxious and uncertain. Should he touch the timer? Sonia hadn't thought she should. What would happen if he did?

When he went towards the timer it was glowing. He stood and looked at it and then phoned Sonia. She was in her car and said she would come over but had no real idea what to do.

Jason put the coffee pot on, for something practical to do, and Catherine found him in the kitchen. 'So that'll solve everything will it? Coffee is the panacea for all ills. I thought you were fetching the timer. I'll get it.'

'No, Catherine, please don't touch it while it's working.' He grabbed her arm to stop her but she pulled away and ran into the hall. He ran after her but was too late. He saw her touch the glowing timer and she disappeared.

Chapter 25

India

Catherine felt extremely sick. Was it something she ate? She opened her eyes, expecting to see her bedroom but she was inside a tent, lying on a camp bed. If she sat up her nausea might erupt into retching so she lay still, listening. There were cries and moans of people in pain with soothing female voices and over everything the hum of flies. It sounded as if she was in hospital but there was no smell of disinfectant. Her nose twitched with disgust as she recognised the smells of faeces, urine, blood and sweat. She was too hot and flicked the blanket off.

'Hello, are you feeling better, memsahib?'

'Yes, thank you. I'm really thirsty. Do you have any water?' The Indian woman poured water into a tin mug and held it out to her. Catherine drank it greedily despite the earthy taste. 'That's better. I'm not used to this heat.'

'Would you like help getting up?'

'No, I can do it but I don't know where I am.'

'We are camped about ten miles from Lucknow. It is under siege and the women are tending to the sick and injured. Perhaps, when you are dressed, you might be able to help for there are many ill people.'

'Yes, I'm happy to help but I have no clothes.'

'These may fit you, given by the other ladies. Do you need help dressing?'

'No, I can do it, thank you. You don't have to stay with me but before you go do you know a woman called Izzy, Isabelle?'

'There are many white ladies and she may be here but I do not know her.'

She went out of the tent and Catherine got out of the bed and looked at the clothes. They were not very clean but better than nothing. She put them on and ventured outside. It was no cooler and she looked around at the orderly row of tents. Somewhere in the distance she could here the booms of cannons but where was Izzy?

She walked along following the moans of the wounded. Izzy would be helping, she was certain of that.

There was a much larger tent and all the sides were rolled up to allow what little air there was. Catherine paused, frightened of what she was going to see. Her basic first aid had not covered drastic wounds.

A woman ran up to her with a bandage in her hand. 'Please help the man in bed twenty-three. He needs his dressing changed and I'm helping the surgeon.'

There was no option now so she followed the chalked numbers on the bottom of the beds and walked along until she found him. When she looked at him she wanted to run away. He had no foot and his bandages were filthy. This was the worst injury she had ever had to deal with. He really needed help and everyone else was busy. She took a deep breath and introduced herself. 'Hello, I'm Catherine Brownlow.'

'I'm Sergeant Makepeace, nurse.' He gave a twisted grin. 'Forgive me if I don't get up.'

Catherine smiled back. 'I have to change your dressing, sergeant, and it's going to hurt.'

'You just do it nurse. I don't want gangrene.'

The bandage was stiff with blood and difficult to unwind. It would come away better if she could wet it. She looked around and saw a pitcher of water. Now she concentrated on removing the bandage as gently as possible until the stump was revealed. Nausea threatened her again but the wound was clean and there was no rank smell coming from it. She used the new bandage and wrapped it around as best she could. 'No sign of gangrene, sergeant, it's healing well.' He nodded, sighed and closed his eyes. What should she do next?

A soldier was calling for water so she took the pitcher and found a mug. As she held it to his lips she saw another woman at the next bed. Their eyes met. It was Izzy.

Catherine put the mug down and went to Izzy and they hugged tightly.

'Mum, I'm so glad you're here.'

'We were worried when you didn't come back. I touched the timer and woke up in a tent.'

'It's a bit of a shock isn't it?' Their reunion was interrupted by the sound of horses and wagons and shouts from outside. 'It's more wounded men. We have to put up more camp beds and sort them into too ill to survive, needing surgery or just stitching and dressing. Come on.'

The scene outside was appalling. Men were piled onto carts their wounds bleeding through crude bandages some in silent agony while others screamed. Soldiers lifted the men down and placed them on the ground and the women sorted them into the three categories. More camp beds were erected and eventually the chaos had a semblance of order.

Catherine and Izzy had no medical skill so they fetched and carried as necessary with no rest or food until it began to get dark. They ate ravenously when the food arrived but as soon as that need was satisfied they sat together to talk.

'Your Dad said the timer has something for you to achieve. Do you know what that is?' asked Mum.

'Not yet but it obviously has something to do with Jane who is sitting over there in the grey dress with her maid Emily and our little friend, Mary, and her family. She keeps looking at us and I will need to introduce you to her so we have to invent a story. Jane thinks I had some traumatic experience that wiped my memory. Any ideas?'

'It will be easier if we tell her that I'm your mother and have been looking for you since we were attacked. She's coming over so that will have to do.'

Jane arrived smiling, held out her hand to Catherine and introductions and explanations were made.

'How wonderful that you've found each other again,' said Jane. I wish I could find my husband. They tell me his regiment is in Lucknow, fighting and every time the wounded are brought to us I look for him. When he's not there I don't know whether I'm relieved or not.' She rubbed her back and Catherine asked if she had backache and would she like to sit down.

'It's been aching all day and sitting does seem to ease it for a while. Did you have the same when you were in an interesting condition?'

'I did towards the end when I was very large but you're still quite small,' replied Catherine. 'I think you should try and rest more but I realise it's not easy to do that in the midst of a war.'

'You have made me realise how tired I feel now so, please forgive me if I retire to bed. Oh, Isabelle, you will probably want to move your things out of my tent to be with your mother. Let's do that now.' They walked together and soon all the women were reorganised and in bed.

'Do you think we have any hope of going home in our sleep?' asked Catherine.

'I don't think so, Mum. It seems we are stuck until we solve whatever it is but I'm really glad to be sharing it with you.'

Chapter 26

England

The doorbell rang and Jason welcomed Sonia in. They hugged and then he led her into the kitchen.

'I think I'll have my coffee black today. I feel a need for undiluted caffeine,' said Sonia.

Jason poured the coffee and they sat cradling the hot mugs and for a moment it was silent. Jason pushed a packet of biscuits towards her but she shook her head.

'So, where is the timer?'

'It's in a cardboard box in the hall. You walked by it when you came in.'

'I assume it's glowing.' Jason nodded. 'And they're both in India during the mutiny.'

Jason nodded and explained Catherine's fear when she realised Izzy was still in the past. 'She got really agitated and before I could stop her she touched the timer and disappeared.'

'I've said before that the timer will not harm a woman so that's one comforting thought but I don't have many options. If one of us touched it we could go too and that wouldn't solve anything. Oh I've just thought. Does Izzy have to work today?'

'Yes, this afternoon, I'd forgotten. I'll ring the store now and say she's sick.'

He returned a few minutes later looking sheepish. 'I hate lying but could hardly tell them the truth. Have you told Roger where you are?'

'No, he thinks I've gone shopping for clothes so he won't worry about me until late this afternoon. Mind you he'll be suspicious if I go home empty handed because that never happens.'

He smiled, recognising her attempt to lighten the situation but he felt anxious and helpless.

'I wish I could think of something practical to do that might help. Did I tell you Izzy said Jane was pregnant?' Sonia shook her head and he continued. 'The thing is the family tree says she died without having any children so perhaps that's significant.

'You could be right. What would happen to all the changes we made using the timer if Jane had the baby and stayed in India?'

Jason stood up and poured some more coffee. 'I don't know. It makes me scared. Nathan disappeared, never to have existed. That could happen to Izzy and Catherine. They might never return. My God, what have we done?'

He sat down abruptly and held his head in his hands. When she saw tears dripping onto the table Sonia got up and put her arms around him. 'We must put our faith in the timer protecting women. We've no choice but to wait, hope and pray.' She held onto him until he stirred and searched for a tissue. 'I think we should do something practical to pass the time,' said Sonia.

'Like what?'

'Well it's a lovely sunny day so let's do some gardening; that's what we need.'

'The hedge at the bottom could do with a trim. I was going to do it before we went away but didn't get around to it. I'll get the hedge trimmer out of the shed and you can be chief 'pick upperer'. Jason stood abruptly, collected the key to the shed and went outside. She washed the cups and heard the trimmer start; her cue to go and join him but then the doorbell rang. She answered the door and saw a handsome young man smiling at her.

'Hello, I assume you're Izzy's mum back from your cruise. I wonder if I could see Izzy because she hasn't been answering my texts.'

'Oh, er, come in.' He did so and she shut the door behind him before saying, 'so you're a friend of Izzy?'

'Sorry my name's Andrew. I knew Izzy when we were at school and met her a week or so ago and we've become friends. Is she here?' Sonia beckoned him to follow her to the kitchen. 'I'm not Catherine, Izzy's mum; I'm a friend of the family, Sonia. Catherine and Izzy have gone to see a sick relative and could be away for a couple of days.'

'Well why didn't she tell me? She must have a dozen texts from me. I don't understand it. We were getting on so well. It's a mean way to dump me.'

'Don't assume that, please. It was very sudden and it's possible she left without her phone.' He looked doubtful at that but she added, hastily, 'Let me go and have a look in her bedroom.'

Sonia ran up the stairs, worried that Jason might come into the kitchen and their stories might not corroborate. The phone was obvious, on the bedside cabinet, so she grabbed it and ran back down arriving out of breath. She showed it to him, saying, 'That's why you've had no response. Izzy would never just keep silent if she wanted to break off a relationship. She would tell you to your face.'

'Well, I'll just have to wait until she gets back then.' He stood up to go and Sonia showed him to the door. He mumbled his thanks and she shut it behind him, releasing her breath in an audible sigh. She could hear the whirr of the hedge trimmer and went into the garden to tell Jason of this latest complication.

They worked together until lunchtime and then stopped and admired their work. The hedge was straight at the top, neat along the sides and the trimmings bagged, ready to go to the tip for recycling. It was enough for one session so Jason put the tools away and they returned to the kitchen. Indoors the tension of waiting grew again.

'Sonia I think you should go home or pop into town and buy something so Roger doesn't get suspicious. You can do nothing here but I'm really grateful for your help.'

'Ok I'll go shopping but please ring me when they come home or if you want me to hold your hand again.' They both smiled, stood up and he gave her a long hug before she left.

India

Izzy was dreaming of Andrew when Emily woke her. 'Memsahib, the baby is coming.'

'Tell Jane I'm on my way.' She woke her mum and they both dressed quickly.

'I hope you know something about having babies, Mum, 'cause I don't.'

'I only have my experience of having you and we've both watched those old dvds of 'Call the Midwife.' Izzy smiled at that and they hurried towards Jane's tent. They could hear her moaning

160

and Emily trying to sooth her before they opened the flap. Both women looked relieved to see Catherine and Izzy.

'Do you know how long it has been between contractions?' asked Catherine.

'They shook their heads and then Jane said, 'We don't have any kind of timepiece here.' Catherine was annoyed with herself for asking the question and said, 'When you get the next one Izzy can do a steady count then we'll have some idea how close you are. Emily we will want to wash the baby and Jane after the birth and hot water is better. Could you do that?' Emily nodded and she went out.

Jane moaned with pain and Izzy quietly counted and got to one hundred and eighty before she moaned again. 'Mum, that's just three minutes. It's getting close. Do you think we should ask the doctor to come?'

Catherine shook her head as she wiped Jane's face and neck with a damp cloth. 'That poor man needs his sleep. Let's wait and call him if there seems to be a problem.'

'You're very calm, Mum. I'm so glad you're here.'

'Amen to that,' said Jane just as another spasm waved in. 'Oh God this is almost unbearable. Do you have any laudanum?'

'I'll go to the medical tent and ask. They're bound to have some,' said Izzy glad to be on a mission and away from the tension for a while. She asked a nurse and was told to ask the surgeon. He was in the midst of an operation and she felt uncomfortable asking but felt she must.

'Sorry, I can't spare laudanum for childbirth. We have limited supplies and it must be used for operations. Whatever she's going through it's nothing compared to the agony of these men.' Izzy, suitably chastened, went back to break the news to Jane. She took it well.

It was hard watching her suffer. When the contractions became fiercer she threw away her inhibitions and screamed. Throughout Catherine was calm and when the urge to push arrived she got Izzy to help support Jane's upper body as she watched the slow but steady emergence of the head. Suddenly, with one louder scream, the head was in Catherine's hands. 'You're nearly there. Give it all you've got on the next contraction and it will be over.'

Jane obeyed, without screaming and her son was born. Catherine then began to panic because she didn't know what to do with the cord. What could she cut it with? How did you seal it? 'Izzy go and see if the doctor could spare us just a couple of minutes and get him to bring sterile scissors or a scalpel.'

He had just finished the operation and was washing his hands. 'Yes, I'll come and do that. What's the patient's name?'

'Jane, Jane Carstairs.'

'That name's familiar. I think I treated an officer with that name.'

'It could be her husband, Cecil. He's been fighting in Lucknow.'

'Well that's good because he's still alive and it would help him greatly to know his wife and...'

'Baby boy,' Izzy said quickly.

'Good,' said the doctor again as they walked to Jane's tent. He finished the job efficiently coming just in time to deal with the afterbirth and then left the ladies to use the hot water. He left without mentioning the possibility of Cecil being in the hospital and Izzy decided to keep quiet for the time being. Jane was exhausted and needed to sleep. They left Emily cradling the baby and sitting beside Jane.

When they were back in their own tent Catherine told Mum what the doctor had said.

'That's fantastic news, Izzy, but I think it might be good to ask about his injuries and his chances of recovery before we tell her. I'm starving now. Let's see if we can find some breakfast.'

It was an hour later when they reported for duty in the hospital tent after first checking that Jane and her son were still sleeping. The doctor was sitting down amongst the chaos of bloody bandages and cradling a cup of tea. His face was grey with exhaustion and when he looked up at their approach his eyes were red rimmed.

'How's our baby and mother faring?'

'They're both fine, sir, doing better than you if I may say so.'

'Yes I've not slept for two days and nights but it's quiet now so I'm off to bed for a few hours.' He stood up and neither woman could bring herself to ask about Cecil Carstairs. Then a nurse bustled up and gave them work to do and it was only by chance that Izzy

162

found him. She had been asked to change a dressing on a sabre wound that had been stitched and the man was awake and sitting up.

'Good morning sir, my name is Isabelle and I have to change your dressing.'

'If you must then go ahead.' He pulled back the covers to reveal a huge gash in his thigh. 'The surgeon said he was surprised I didn't die of blood loss before I got here but I was lucky to have a friend who knew how to use a tourniquet. Sorry I'm forgetting my manners. I'm Captain Carstairs.' He must have thought her crazy as she smiled broadly and held out her hand.

'I'm really pleased to meet you. I know your wife Jane. We travelled together.'

'Did she get to Calcutta and get on the ship?'

'No and it's a long story that she'll tell you herself because she's here in the camp.' She saw his face change with different emotions – anger and confusion.

'It was not her fault. We met the army coming to relieve Lucknow and we were made to travel with them.' He still looked agitated but she needed to calm him so she blurted out. 'It was good that she was here last night where we had a doctor because she has just given birth to your son.'

The poor man could no longer cope, probably in pain and receiving such news and tears ran down his cheeks. 'A son, I have a son. Is Jane well?'

'She was asleep when I saw her this morning and Emily's with her. She will be so pleased to know you're here and alive. Before she can come and see you she must get her strength back and I must change your dressing.'

Izzy had dressed several wounds by this time and her bandaging skills were improving. When she had finished and covered him up he sank back, tired with the pain and effort. 'Thank you, Isabelle. Please tell my wife I'm delighted and want to see her as soon as she's recovered.' He closed his eyes and Izzy moved away looking for Mum to tell her the news.

Chapter 27

England

Jason was desperate to keep active and when Sonia left he went for a run and thought about Catherine's family tree. Perhaps it had changed and then he'd know they were achieving something. Perhaps they were already home and he wasn't there. He turned without pausing and ran back home as fast as he could. He opened the front door and knew, by the heavy silence and the faint glow from the timer in the box, they were still in the past.

He sighed, walked into the kitchen and boiled the kettle. He was hungry and made himself a cheese sandwich taking it into the den to eat. He looked at the family tree, scrolled down while bringing his sandwich to his mouth but put it back on the plate. 'Woah, Jane had a baby, Mark. He died after Jane and never married or had any children. They've changed something so why are they still there?' He looked again and saw that her husband had died a few days after his son was born. 'They've got to save him before the timer brings them back.'

He sat eating without tasting and was surprised when he saw his empty plate. There had to be something he could do. If he touched the timer he might find himself in India but would have trouble explaining his modern clothes and anyway what could he do to help?

He knew nothing about being a soldier but the waiting was becoming unbearable. He ran back to the computer and looked up soldier's uniforms in 1857.

It seemed khaki had been introduced for some Indian regiments and enterprising English soldiers had dyed their conspicuous white summer uniforms with tea. He ran upstairs and found a short sleeved, khaki shirt and similar colour tracksuit. They were too clean but there was plenty of dirt in the garden.

In just a few minutes he was dressed in soiled clothes, wearing scuffed black boots and standing by the box, uncertain. Supposing he went somewhere else? He was just assuming Izzy and Catherine were together. 'Oh, sod it,' he said and picked up the timer.

India

Jason opened his eyes and shut them again. He felt sick and it was dark. He turned over to get more comfortable and realised he had no pillow and the bed was hard and full of grit. It took him a while to realise he was on the floor and it felt like dried mud.

I needn't have taken the trouble to make my clothes dirty, he thought. Then he became wide awake and sat up. His head felt heavy and nausea was still there but he needed to know if he was in India. Gradually his senses became aware of moans, a baby was crying and there was an unpleasant stench. He rolled onto his hands and knees and stood up, carefully. His eyes were now accustomed to the dark and he moved towards a camp bed. As he leaned over it a fist shot up and hit him full in the face. He stumbled back with shock and pain as Catherine yelled, 'Get away from me. Izzy, help!'

For a moment all was chaos as Izzy moved quickly ready to attack the intruder, only to find him opening his arms to give her a hug.

'Perhaps you'll give me a better greeting than Mum. She's just hit me with a right hook.'

'Dad. What are you doing here?' Catherine joined the family hug and they all began to talk at once. Then they stopped, laughed, and Catherine said, 'You go first Jason.'

He told them about his fears and Sonia's visit. When he mentioned Andrew's visit Izzy stopped his flow.

'Oh he must be wondering why I've stopped texting. He probably thinks I don't want to see him any more and I really do.'

'Don't worry Sonia said you and Mum had gone on an urgent visit to help a sick relative.'

'What, without my phone? He'd know I'd never do that.'

'Sorry, Izzy , it was the best Sonia could think of quickly but she did fetch your phone and show him.'

He finished his story with the certainty they needed to protect Cecil.

'He's here, Dad, wounded with a sabre cut but it doesn't seem life threatening, unless he gets an infection and I don't see how we can stop that. They don't have antibiotics.'

'I don't know either. Do you two help in the hospital?'

'Yes,' they both said together and laughed again.

'Do you think I could help and not be noticed too much?'

Izzy had an idea. 'We can bandage you so you look like a recovering patient. They do help, especially when we get a new wave of wounded men.'

Izzy frequently had the job of soaking and then boiling used bandages and had a pile in the tent ready to go back to the hospital. Dawn was breaking as she bandaged his left arm, put it in a sling and then, for good measure put one around his head.

'There I think you'll pass.'

'You're getting very good at that,' said Mum. 'It's getting light and I think we should be finding some breakfast. When you go into the hospital tent find a chair and try to look miserable. Breakfast will be brought to you, eventually.'

They left the tent together and Jason walked slowly into the hospital tent. People were only just beginning to wake up and there were calls for bedpans and pee bottles. Jason sat down, watched what a nurse did and then copied her. She passed him, paused and Jason thought he'd been discovered as an imposter but she just gave him a tired smile and said, 'Thank you.'

As he moved around he checked the names and eventually found Captain Cecil Carstairs. 'Do you need a bottle, bed pan, water sir?'

'No thank you the nurse saw to my needs and I might be getting up today.'

'That's good, sir. I'll help if you need someone to lean on.' Cecil smiled and nodded. He really seemed in good shape thought Jason as he moved on to the next bed.

Breakfast arrived an hour later on a trolley. Jason noticed a pile of chapattis' and a steaming bowl that had a spicy smell. It was being served by an Indian soldier who kept his back towards Jason. He appeared to be talking to each patient for the response was a grunt or even a cry of pain.

Jason watched him working his way down the long row of beds and noticed that none of the men who had been given food were trying to eat. They must need help to sit up or need someone to feed them. It was bad enough to be injured without starving too. He got up and as he passed the soldier who was serving the food he kept his head down, not wanting to be recognised as an imposter.

166

He reached the patient in the first bed. He seemed to be asleep and, not wanting to wake him, Jason moved to the next. He was asleep too. Both men seemed to have fresh blood on their dressings. Perhaps he should tell the doctor but the surgeon was busy behind a mosquito net. When Jason moved to the third man and saw the same scenario he examined him closer. He was not breathing. Looking back at the other two he saw they were also dead. Finally it occurred to him that the Indian soldier was delivering food with a very sharp stiletto.

Jason had never hit anyone in anger. His reaction was instinctive as he ran down the ward just as the silent murderer reached Cecil's bed. A rugby tackle brought him down and the knife flew from his hand. There was a scrabble for it and Jason won. For a moment he thought to treat the man to his own medicine wanting to plunge it into his back but the noise had brought men and nurses running. Someone disarmed Jason and in the confusion both men were restrained.

'The white man saved my life!' shouted Cecil. 'That murdering bastard has been killing everyone.' Jason's arms were released and he stood unsteady with shock. Everyone rushed around him checking the dead soldiers and moving them out of the tent. Catherine and Izzy arrived in the chaos and they joined in helping, not registering him in their haste. Jason moved towards Cecil and sat down.

'I didn't realise what he was doing. I should have moved quicker and perhaps I could have saved more men. What a senseless, cruel thing to do.'

'This war has seen much more cruel and senseless acts than that. At least he despatched them swiftly, with one blow. But why am I telling you that? You're a soldier after all. What regiment are you in?' asked Cecil.

Jason had no idea how to answer that question but was saved by the arrival of Izzy and Catherine.

'I heard you were a hero, Dad.' Jason smiled and Cecil looked oddly at him.

'Dad?'

Catherine laughed. 'This is quite a family affair, Captain. We all got separated in a skirmish and have met here. Rather similar to your wife being here and having her baby. Jane is feeling much better today and has asked if you are well enough to see her.'

Catherine's skilful mention of his wife and child stopped Cecil from asking any more awkward questions and he smiled. 'I think I can do better than that. I was told I could get up today so I will see if I can walk to see her. He looked at Jason. Would you help me?'

'I'd be delighted. He helped Cecil stand and while he was doing that Catherine and Jane rushed out of the tent to warn Jane and to make sure she was ready to receive him. Emily combed her mistress' hair and placed the sleeping baby in Jane's arms as the two men arrived. Jason stepped away and Catherine, Izzy and Emily left too, to give the happy couple their special moment alone.

'I'm starving. I never got any breakfast and it's been an exciting start to the day,' said Jason. 'I wonder why we're still here? Surely we've finished the task.' There was no answer as he saw Izzy fade and disappear and then Catherine did the same. They've gone back but what about me. He raised his hands as he thought that and saw them fading and he knew no more.

England

Sonia was calling their names but she was so far away. Catherine tried to open her eyes but it was too much effort. She gave up and said, 'I'd die for a cup of tea.'

'I've brought you both one but Jason seems out for the count.' Sonia watched as Catherine dragged herself to a sitting position and reached for her tea. 'That's sheer heaven, thanks, Sonia. What are you doing here?'

'Well it's probably difficult for you to understand but you've been gone for five days and I've been going mad with worry.'

'Five days?' Catherine was now wide-awake. I'm sorry, Sonia. I was so involved I'd no idea of time or what was happening here. Izzy, is she back too?'

'Yes she's drinking her tea, awake and already sending texts to Andrew.'

'That's good.' She threw back the covers and looked ruefully at her filthy clothes. I'm starving. Have we any food? I fancy eggs and bacon and loads of toast.' Sonia smiled. 'I can organise that while you get dressed but you may like to know it's lunch time, not early morning.'

'It doesn't matter I'm just so pleased to be home. If you start cooking I'll give Jason a shove and then have a shower. I think I stink.' She giggled and Sonia laughed with her.

She went downstairs and found Izzy dressed and looking at her phone. 'Is that Andy?'

'Yes. We need to agree on the story that I went to see a sick relative who is now better. He's meeting me tonight to take me out to dinner. There's no way I could tell him the truth. He'd think me crazy.'

'Yes, it's not easy,' said Sonia. 'I never told Roger anything last time for the same reason. I'm cooking egg and bacon. Would you like some?'

Izzy smiled and nodded her fingers tapping on the phone. Finally she stood up and went into the hall. 'It's gone! Sonia, Mum, Dad the timer's gone, disappeared.'

Dad stumbled down the stairs still in filthy clothes and stared into the box as if he expected it to reappear. Then he went into the study and opened Catherine's family tree. Everyone crowded around, with a few comments about his smell, but all anxious to see the changes.

'We did it! Look, Cecil outlived both his son and his wife. He died quite an old man at seventy-five. No other children or grandchildren so we've hurt no one. Excellent!

'So when are you going to tell me what happened, exactly?' asked Sonia.

'Catherine and Izzy can relate everything while I get cleaned up and can I have two eggs please, as I'm a superhero.' He laughed and went upstairs.

When he returned, his hair still damp, Sonia and Catherine were dishing up a feast while Izzy was balancing more toast onto a plate already piled high. They all sat down and Jason lifted his glass of orange juice.

'Let's have a toast to the end of our adventures and Catherine's happy ancestors.'

They clinked glasses and began to eat.

Sources

The Indian Mutiny by John Harris

Harrogate Herald on microfiche at Harrogate Library

About the Author

I was born in London in 1946, the middle child of three. The family moved to Harlow in Essex when it was a very small, new town with an enthusiastic community spirit.

I went to S. Martin's College of education and became a primary school teacher, returning to Harlow for my first job. The following year I married John, we moved to Biggleswade in Bedfordshire and, during the next seven years, our two children were born. During this time I studied with the Open University and gained a BA.

John was offered a promotion if he would move to North Yorkshire. He accepted with pleasure, having had many camping holidays in the area. The gentler pace of life was good for growing children and for a writer.

Writing has always been something I enjoyed, poems, stories and holiday diaries but, when I took early retirement, I went to a creative writing class. Out of that a self-help group was formed called The Next Chapter. We wrote stories and poems but were all excited when a local author suggested a course called, 'Write a book in a Year'. I wrote my first novel, 'Forced To Flee' about the ethnic cleansing of Albanians in Kosovo, during the collapse of Yugoslavia.

There was still a need to write and, as I have enjoyed many fantasy stories, 'Pathway Back' became my next project. Whilst writing both novels I have been creating a memoir so keep an eye open for, 'When Life throws you a Lemon.'